A F

MW00479842

Dune House Cozy Mystery Series

Cindy Bell

Copyright © 2016 Cindy Bell

All rights reserved.

ISBN-13: 978-1533006578

ISBN-10: 1533006571

More Cozy Mysteries by Cindy Bell

Dune House Cozy Mysteries

Seaside Secrets

Boats and Bad Guys

Treasured History

Hidden Hideaways

Dodgy Dealings

Suspects and Surprises

Ruffled Feathers

Sage Gardens Cozy Mysteries

Birthdays Can Be Deadly

Money Can Be Deadly

Trust Can Be Deadly

Ties Can Be Deadly

Rocks Can Be Deadly

Jewelry Can Be Deadly

Chocolate Centered Cozy Mysteries

The Sweet Smell of Murder

A Deadly Delicious Delivery

A Bitter Sweet Murder

A Treacherous Tasty Trail

Table of Contents

Chapter One

Mary drank in the sweet sound of Summer's laughter. Sometimes she forgot that the medical examiner was still a young woman. As she studied the assortment of fabrics that Suzie spread out before her, it was clear that she was excited about her upcoming wedding.

"I can't thank you enough for allowing us to have the wedding here."

"Are you kidding?" Suzie smiled. "I wouldn't let you have it anywhere else. There are plenty of rooms for all of your out-of-town guests, and we can convert the living area into a nice buffet and bar. We'll work hard to make sure it will be perfect for you."

"It's going to be perfect, as long as Jason shows up."

Mary raised an eyebrow. "Are you concerned

about that?"

"Not really. I mean, doesn't every bride worry a little?"

"I wouldn't know." Suzie grinned.

"I did." Mary laughed. "Right up until the moment that I saw him at the end of the aisle. A million things run through your mind, and it's all normal."

"Still, you don't need to worry. My cousin is an amazing young man, and quite dependable. He will be there, barring some disaster," Suzie said.

"Oh please, don't even say that." Summer shook her head and looked back at the fabrics before her. "It's hard enough to pick out a tablecloth, I don't want to even think about disasters."

"It's all going to be just fine." Mary patted the back of her hand. "I can tell you this much, you're not going to remember what color your tablecloths were or how many times you stutter during your vows. All you're going to remember is that perfect moment, when you look into each others' eyes and promise to be together for the rest of your lives. It's that moment that counts."

"I keep trying to tell myself that, but then something reminds me of things I haven't even thought about and I start to panic."

"No need to panic, we're here to help you, Summer. Anything you're worried about, you just let us know."

"Thanks so much." She sighed with relief. "I'm so lucky to have the two of you to give me some help with all of this. My mother isn't really interested in organizing a wedding. She is happy I'm marrying Jason, but she doesn't know what all of the fuss is about."

"We're honored to be part of it all." Suzie ran her gaze over a list of different tasks that needed to be completed. "By the way, Paul's friend, Robbie, should be docking today or tomorrow. We will be meeting with him to organize the amount of shellfish we will need for the wedding. If we add that to the fish Paul will supply, we're going to have plenty of food."

"Fantastic. I love the idea of offering a local buffet," Summer said. "I arranged with the butcher in town to get some chicken and beef as well so there is a variety, and in case there is anyone who doesn't like seafood."

"Good idea." Mary nodded and pointed to a white, linen tablecloth with small roses embroidered on the edge. "This one is pretty."

"Yes it is, but it seems a bit flowery," Summer said. "I was thinking something a bit more nautical would be nice."

"Maybe this one?" Suzie dug through the pile of samples and showed her a white tablecloth with wavy blue stripes along the edges. "Will it compliment the centerpieces?"

"The centerpieces." Summer's eyes widened. "I haven't even thought about them!" Panic caused her voice to grow shrill.

"Relax, we have plenty of time to put them together. Remember, decorating is my specialty. Let me pull up some ideas so that you can start to think about what you might like." Suzie picked up her cell phone and began sorting through different options. She tagged a few that she thought Summer might like.

"What about the cake? Where are you with that?" Mary leaned closer to her.

"I know that I'm going to use the bakery in town. I know it's just going to be two tiers and I've narrowed it down to four flavors, but Jason is supposed to make the final decision. He has been so busy since Kirk has been off on medical leave that he's barely had a chance to choose anything with me."

"I'll make sure he gets there this afternoon, that way the baker will have enough time to prepare the cake," Suzie said.

"Good luck. That's why I'm a little concerned about him showing up for the wedding. At this point we're not even sure that he's going to be off duty on the day of the wedding."

"Are you serious?" Mary gasped. "That needs to be settled."

"I know, I know. But he keeps telling me his boss is trying to get someone to come in from Parish. So far it hasn't been confirmed."

"I'm sure they'll find someone." Mary smiled at her. "Just take a deep breath. By the end of today we'll have the tablecloths picked out, the centerpieces narrowed down, and Jason will choose a cake. Right Suzie?"

"Absolutely." Suzie nodded, then looked into Summer's eyes. "We are in this together, sweetie. Your job is to stress as little as possible."

"I'm trying." She grinned and began to look through the options on Suzie's phone. Suzie glanced at her watch. Paul was due to arrive at the dock around four, and she couldn't wait. As accustomed as she was to him being out on the water, she still counted down the hours to when

6

he would be back. It wasn't so much that she missed him, but that she wanted to hear about his experiences out on the open water. He was so passionate when he spoke about them, and his skin always smelled like the ocean for a few days when he returned.

"What do you think about this one, Suzie?" Summer pointed out one of the centerpieces.

"Sure, that would be simple to do. I'll head out and pick out some supplies. You two finish choosing the table settings. Okay?"

"Thank you so much, Suzie." Summer handed her back her phone.

"I'm happy to do it." Suzie winked at her then waved to Mary. She grabbed her purse on the way to the door.

The moment Suzie stepped outside she was greeted by bright sunshine. She squinted against it for a moment, then allowed it to wash over her. The view from Dune House was always a welcome sight. She looked back at the beautiful bed and breakfast by the sea and smiled. Running Dune House filled her with a sense of belonging that she had never experienced anywhere else. As she walked to her car she scanned the horizon for any sign of Paul's boat. It was still early, but it didn't hurt to look. Only flat open sea was in sight. At least it was a calm day.

Suzie drove towards town and parked in front of the craft supplies store. By the time she had everything that she needed it was close to three. She walked a few blocks down to the bakery. As soon as she arrived she placed a call to Jason.

"Something very suspicious is happening at the bakery. Can you please come and check it out."

"Suzie, are you okay?"

"Yes, but please come and have a look around." She hung up the phone before he could say anything else.

Minutes later the siren of a patrol car wailed down the street. Jason pulled to a stop in front of the shop.

8

"Suzie? Is everything okay?" He jumped out of the car and rushed towards her.

"Everything is fine." She smiled. "Now that you're here."

"What?" He glanced around for any sign of trouble.

"It's time to pick a cake, Jason."

"Suzie, I'm on duty." He frowned.

"You're always on duty. Summer needs you, too."

"I just can't right now, I'm too busy. You really shouldn't have placed a call like that."

"Really? Are there that many calls flooding the police station right now?"

"Well no."

"You have your radio on, don't you?"

"Yes." He adjusted it on his hip. "I guess I could spare a few minutes."

"It's important to show Summer just how

important she and this wedding are to you. So, I think it would be best if you took the time to get this settled. If I have to pin you down and force the cake into your mouth myself, I will. You know that I will."

"Okay, okay, that will not be necessary." He opened the door to the bakery. "Let's pick a cake."

Suzie followed him into the bakery. She was going to make sure that he followed through with a choice so that Summer didn't have to worry anymore. But as she glanced over at him she was a little worried. His skin was pale, his eyes had fairly dark circles beneath them, and his general attitude was more sour than usual.

He gestured to the woman behind the counter. "I'd like to pick a wedding cake please. My fiancée, Summer Rose, said you would have a few samples for me to choose from."

"Are you doing okay, Jason?" Suzie asked as the bakery assistant organized the cakes.

"Sure." He nodded.

"I know this has to be hard for you with your parents gone."

"Suzie, I'm fine. I'm just a little worn out from pulling all of these extra shifts. Kirk picked the wrong time to get appendicitis."

"That's for sure." Suzie shook her head. "But don't worry we have everything for the wedding under control."

"The shellfish?"

"We are arranging it today."

"Good. I'm glad to hear it. Summer's family loves shellfish. You know I'm grateful for everything that you and Mary are doing to help us out."

"We're grateful to be there for the both of you. Plus, the photographs will be perfect for the wedding brochure."

"I'm not exactly model material."

"You're far more handsome than you give yourself credit for."

"I don't know about all that." He smiled as four small plates were placed in front of him.

"There's several different kinds of frosting we can do as well."

"Something light and creamy." He picked up a fork. "You're going to help me choose, right Suzie?"

"Absolutely." She laughed and picked up a fork as well. Four small slices of cake later she waddled out of the bakery with Jason. "I'm glad you found one you like."

"I just hope that it is the one that Summer liked the most, too."

"Either way you know she will like it. She'll also be very relieved to know that you ordered the cake."

Just as he opened the door to the patrol car his radio began to chatter. "Right on time." He laughed and shook his head. "Back to work."

"Thanks, Jason."

He waved to her as he drove away. Instead of walking back towards her car Suzie headed for the docks. If Paul wasn't in yet he would be in soon. When she approached the dock she was pleased to see that his boat was in the slip.

"Paul?" She smiled as she boarded the boat. "Paul?"

"How I have missed that voice!" He chuckled as he emerged from the small cabin. "I was just going to call you. How did you know I was in?"

"I just thought I'd take a chance." She offered him a light kiss. "Good trip?"

"Yes. I got quite a haul and the weather was nice. Too nice."

"Why do you say that?"

"Oh, you know, calm before the storm. Too much good weather worries me sometimes."

"Hopefully it will be nice for the wedding."

"How are the plans coming along?" He grabbed a rag from the cabin and began wiping down the railings on the boat.

"Pretty good. The couple is nervous which is to be expected."

"I'm sure it will be perfect with you and Mary at the helm. Oh, look at that." He pointed further down the dock. "Looks like Robbie is already in. That's odd, I thought he would let me know when he got close."

"Should we go say hi?"

"Sure. I can't wait for him to meet you properly." Suzie had only been introduced to him in passing, they had never had time to stop and have a conversation. "I only really know him from the docks, but he's got great stories. He likes to talk and he's always into something." Suzie knew that Paul was a loner and only had a few friends, most of whom were fishermen.

"Sounds interesting."

He helped her down off the boat then they walked together towards Robbie's boat.

"He's a real good guy, you'll see. Hey look." He shaded his eyes as he looked out over the water. "That's Simon's boat. Simon!" He waved in an attempt to get Simon's attention. The boat continued away from the dock. Suzie expected that the man at the helm could hear Paul's hollering, but he didn't turn to look. Maybe he was busy with something or the noise of the engine drowned out Paul's voice.

"He must be busy." She tugged at his sleeve. "I'm eager to meet the man with so many stories."

"Sure." Paul stared out at the water for a moment longer. "Simon is the one who introduced us actually. Simon and I go way back, and I guess he took Robbie under his wing."

"That was nice of him."

"Nice in some ways. Dangerous in others." Paul chuckled and raised an eyebrow. Before she could question him further about his comment, he paused in front of Robbie's boat. "Robbie?" Paul knocked on the side of the boat. "Are you in there?" He waited a moment for a response. When none came he glanced over at Suzie. "Maybe he went into town for some food." He started to turn away, then stopped. "Hm. That's odd."

"What?" Suzie looked past him at the boat.

"One of the storage bins is unlocked and it's got some shellfish in it," Paul said as he looked inside. "Robbie would never leave it that way. Anyone could just walk up and help themselves."

"Maybe he's inside then and just didn't hear us."

"Maybe." He climbed onto the boat then reached back to help her up. "If not we can just wait for him."

Suzie steadied herself with the railing of the boat and watched as Paul glanced around.

"Robbie? Are you here?" Paul walked towards the cabin. She followed after him as the smell of fish surrounded her. "Robbie, bud, you on the boat?" Paul knocked on the cabin door.

"Paul, look!" Suzie pointed to the bottom corner of the door. "Is that blood?"

"Sure looks like it. Robbie?" He tried to push the door to the cabin open. He got it part of the way open then it hit something hard. "Something is blocking it. Let me see what's in the way." He stuck his head inside and gasped. "Robbie? Robbie? Are you okay?" He crouched down to take a better look. "Suzie, call Jason, call an ambulance."

"What's wrong?" Suzie pulled out her phone and started dialing.

"It's Robbie. I don't think he's breathing." Paul pushed the door the rest of the way open. Suzie caught sight of Robbie's body stretched out across the floor.

Chapter Two

"Suzie, I can't do a fake call right now," Jason said quickly.

"It's not fake I'm afraid. We need police and an ambulance as soon as possible, at the docks. Slip nine."

"I'm heading out right now."

She hung up the phone and squeezed through the door to check on Robbie's vitals. It was easy to see that he was already gone and from the stab wounds it was clear that he had been murdered.

"How did this happen?" Paul stared down at his friend's body.

"Jason is on his way." Suzie shook her head. "He's gone, Paul. I'm sorry." She quickly looked over the cabin as she opened her arms to him.

He shook his head and pulled her back out of the cabin. "I just don't understand how this could happen. Who would want to hurt Robbie?" He stared into her eyes. Suzie recognized the signs of shock in his pale skin and wide eyes.

"Let's get off the boat. Anything we touch can taint the evidence."

"Evidence," he muttered. "He was murdered wasn't he? How could that be? I just spoke to him yesterday."

"You'll need to tell Jason all about that. It's important to try to remember every detail you can."

Relief flooded Suzie when she saw Jason arrive at the docks.

"Suzie? What happened?" He jogged up to the boat. "Are you okay?"

"We're okay, but the captain of the boat is dead." She cringed as she pointed towards the cabin.

"Robbie." Paul shook his head.

"Get on that boat, and take the paramedics." Jason directed another officer. Then he turned back to Paul. "Can you walk me through it?"

"We found him on the boat just about five minutes ago." Paul stared at him with wide, dazed eyes.

"All right just stay right here, I'm going to have some questions for you." Jason looked over at Suzie and nodded.

"We'll be here." Suzie wrapped her arm around Paul's. "Are you doing okay?"

"I'll be fine, as soon as they figure out who did this to Robbie." Paul cleared his throat.

"Look, Jason's coming back." She turned back towards the boat. Jason wore a grave expression as he approached them.

"When was the last time you had contact with Robbie?" He met Paul's eyes.

"Uh, yesterday. It was yesterday. I'd been trying to get hold of him today to see when he planned to dock, but I didn't hear from him."

"And he didn't let you know that he had

docked?"

"Not a text or a radio call. I thought it was odd when I saw his boat in the slip, that's why Suzie and I came over to check it out."

"What about when you boarded the boat? Did you notice anything strange?"

"No, not really." Paul shook his head.

"What about the storage container?" Suzie looked over at him.

"Oh right. Yes, that's why I went looking for him. One of the storage containers was left unlocked. No fisherman leaves one of those unlocked, especially when it has some seafood in it. Anyone could board the boat and take whatever they want."

"Can you show me which one?"

Paul pointed to the container on the boat. "I went to find him because I knew he wouldn't leave the boat like that. But when I tried to get into the cabin." He grimaced.

"We couldn't get the door all the way open, he was in front of the door," Suzie said. "When we went through the small gap it was already too late."

"Maybe, if I had gotten in sooner." Paul frowned. "I don't know."

"There was nothing that you could have done. It looks like he's been gone for at least an hour." Jason met his eyes. "Do you have any idea who might have had a problem with him?"

"With Robbie? No, I'm not sure. I actually haven't seen him in a while. He wasn't exactly the type to make enemies though. I mean he'd get into a bar fight now and then, but most of the time he laughed it off the next day."

"Maybe he crossed someone that didn't find it so amusing?"

"He didn't say anything to me about it. He was his usual cheerful self when I talked to him."

"Cheerful? What does that mean exactly?

What did you talk about?" Jason asked.

Paul sighed. "Just the usual." He glanced over at Suzie.

"Is there a reason you're being evasive with me, Paul?" Jason spread his shoulders and narrowed his eyes.

"Relax Jason, I'm sure he's telling you everything that he knows." Suzie stared at him with a raised eyebrow.

"I think I'll be the judge of that. Paul?" Jason ignored Suzie's stare and focused his attention on Paul.

"Robbie liked to make some off color jokes." Paul frowned. "Not something I'd want to repeat around Suzie. Okay?"

"Oh please, I'm sure I've heard it all, Paul." Suzie rolled her eyes.

"Not from me you haven't, and you won't." He set his jaw.

"Can you give us a minute, Suzie?" Jason

glanced over at her. "Please?"

"Sure." She nodded and released Paul's arm. She moved a few steps away from them and began to scan the dock around her. It was possible Robbie's killer was still nearby. She made a mental note of which boats were docked near Robbie's. A few people gathered at the end of the dock as the police presence became more known. She started to walk towards them to ask some questions, but before she got near them an officer cut in front of her. She sighed and backed off. She didn't want to step on Jason's toes. She turned back towards Paul and noticed that Jason had walked away from him. As she walked back up to him he turned to face her.

"Sorry about that, Suzie."

"I hope you know that you can say anything to me, Paul. I don't care about any off color jokes."

"I just don't think it's appropriate. There are a few things that I am still a little old fashioned about."

"I understand. Did anything he say help Jason?"

"No, I knew that it wouldn't. But you know, Jason, he has to flash his badge."

"Paul."

"I'm sorry, you're right." Paul drew a deep breath. "I'm just a little on edge because of all of this."

"Of course you are. How could you not be? Why don't we go for a drive and try to clear our heads?"

"Yes, I guess that would be best. Jason said he would contact me if he needs anything else."

"Good." Suzie wrapped her arm around his waist and turned him towards the parking lot. "My car is at the bakery."

"Okay. I could use the walk."

Chapter Three

As Suzie and Paul walked towards her car his jaw remained rigid and his eyes sharp as he looked straight forward. When they reached her car she opened the passenger door for him. He barely looked at her as he settled inside. By the time she got around to her side she saw that he hunched forward and hid his face with his hands.

"It's okay, Paul, you have every right to cry." She brushed her hand back through the hair at the nape of his neck.

"Cry?" His voice was muffled by his hands. When he sat up and pulled his hands away she saw his cheeks were bright red, but not a single tear stained his cheeks. "I'm not about to cry, Suzie. I want revenge. I've never wanted it so badly before. Robbie was just a young man. I want to find out who went on his boat and killed him."

"I can see why you're angry." She took his hand in hers and gave it a light squeeze. "I'm angry, too. These things shouldn't happen. Ever. But it has, and the only revenge that we can get is by making sure the murderer is brought to justice."

"How?" Paul shook his head, then stared hard out through the windshield. "What if they never figure out who did this?"

"They will." She gritted her teeth.

"I'm sorry, Suzie. I know you have a lot on your mind with the wedding. I was so looking forward to spending some time with you this evening. But I don't think I'm going to be able to get this off my mind."

"You don't have to. I'm not going to be able to get it off my mind either. If neither of us are going to be able to get it off our minds, then let's see if we can help figure out who killed Robbie ourselves."

"How can you do that with the wedding?"

"I'll make it work. We'd be doing this for

Jason, too. In order for him to concentrate on the wedding and be able to relax and enjoy it, he needs this case wrapped up."

"Good point." Paul nodded. "Where do you want to start?"

"It was pretty clear that Robbie was stabbed. I think we should see what Summer has found out about the body once she's had the chance to examine it. I don't know if she'll tell us anything, but it's worth a shot. I doubt she'll have any information before tomorrow. Until then, let's try to get things back to normal. We can go to get something to eat or just spend some time together. Whatever you're up for."

"Honestly?" He met her eyes.

"Yes of course, honestly."

"I just want some time to clear my head."

"Why don't you sleep at Dune House tonight?"

"No, I want to sleep on my boat."

"Paul, do you think that's a good idea? It could be dangerous."

"I'll be fine. I might be able to get some information out of the guys."

"Do you want me to stay with you on the boat?" Suzie asked.

"No, I think I need some time alone."

"Okay. Why don't I drop you back at your boat? I can spend a little time with Mary, I need to update her anyway."

"Yes, I think that would be best. You don't mind do you?"

"No, not at all. I know that you need some time to sort through this. But call me if you need anything."

"Thank you, Suzie."

As Suzie drove Paul back towards his boat she knew that the best way to help him through this was to help him solve the murder.

When Suzie stopped at the dock the place was

still swarming with police and paramedics. Suzie looked over at Paul.

"Are you sure that you don't want me to stay with you? I could bring you some food by?"

"No, I'll be fine, I promise." He leaned close and kissed her. "Call me as soon as we can get in to see Summer, okay?"

"Sure." She kissed him.

As she watched him walk away from the car she wondered if she should insist on staying by his side. However, she valued her own solitude immensely, and guessed that Paul felt the same way.

Suzie pulled the car back onto the road and focused her attention on the drive back to Dune House. The closer she came to it the calmer she became. It was her place of comfort, where no matter what the problem was, everything seemed to make sense. When she parked she noticed quite a few cars in the lot. Her mind drifted to why they might be there.

Suzie stepped up onto the broad porch of Dune House and took a moment to look out over the outstretched water. The ripple of the wind across its surface stirred up subtle white caps. The calm, clear sky above it was dotted with seabirds. Her heart fluttered at the beauty of it. Yes, there was much to love about life by the sea.

Robbie died on his boat, without even stepping on dry land. The sea could be a wild, unforgiving beast, but it was a human being that could commit murder and the murderer had to be found. She drew a long, slow breath then turned and made her way into Dune House. With the upcoming wedding they hadn't booked in any guests, to keep the rooms open for the wedding guests. However, that did not mean that Dune House was empty. Instead, to her surprise, it bustled with people. Suzie smiled at each person she passed, but didn't stop to talk until she spotted Mary. She stood in the middle of the swarm of people. Her cheeks burned bright red, and her eyes had a slight glaze to them. She was fairly certain that Mary was overwhelmed.

"Mary? What is happening here?" Suzie pressed a hand against her friend's shoulder to get her attention.

"I thought I could get things moving a bit and decided to put a call out there for any assistance from the community. I wasn't expecting such a large response."

"Oh Mary, what a great idea."

"I thought so at the time, but now I wonder if I've just made a bigger mess. No one can agree on anything, and everyone wants to be chosen to provide their service. I think maybe I've gotten in over my head."

"Don't worry, we can get this fixed up. But there's something I need to talk to you about, too."

"Is it about Robbie Stillswell?" Mary met her eyes. "I've heard about that."

"Yes, it is, how did you hear?"

"Gossip travels fast around here." Mary

frowned. "How is Paul?"

"He's okay, but he was shocked, which is to be expected," Suzie said. "He just wanted some space."

"He's a tough guy, Suzie, but he leans on you when he needs to. Don't worry about the wedding, I can handle it."

"I see that." Suzie laughed a little as she looked around at the chaos. "Why don't we get these people organized?"

"I mean it, Suzie, I don't want to pull you away from Paul at a time that he needs you."

"You're not. He sent me away. Besides, this wedding is important to me, too. We won't know anything new about Robbie's death until Summer has a chance to examine him. This will keep me busy."

"Great, because take a look at the centerpieces." She cringed as she pointed to the pile of scraps and glitter. "So far they do not look like the pictures on the website."

"Oh. Why?" Suzie squinted at them.

"Don't ask, just do what you can." Mary grinned and turned to speak to the florist. As Suzie lost herself in the frill and glitter her mind relaxed. The moment it did, the crime scene began to play out in her mind. It was simple to put together what most likely happened. Someone burst into the cabin and attacked Robbie. However, the question of who and why pressed on her until her pulse quickened. It appeared to be someone he was familiar with as there was no evidence of a struggle that she had seen.

Suzie decided that she needed a break. She stood up from the table. Several of the potential suppliers had already left, but a few lingered. Suzie overheard Mary giving specific instructions about what Summer wanted, but she guessed some of it was what Mary wanted. As the last suppliers left Suzie walked over to her.

"How did it go?"

"Well, I think. I'm just not sure if I got my point across. It's so difficult to express to someone just how important a single detail of a single day can be. You know that my marriage didn't turn out the way that I wanted it to, but my wedding day is still a very special memory to me. I'd hate to think of Summer missing out on that memory."

"Or Jason."

"Yes, or Jason. By the way, how did the cake tasting go?"

"He picked a cake. But he's skittish. Not about the wedding. I think he's just stressed from work."

"This murder can't be helping the situation."

"No, I imagine it isn't. He even snapped at Paul."

"Wow. For what?"

"He felt Paul was being evasive. Which he was. But only because there were things he didn't want to say in front of me. He was trying to be a gentleman."

"Ah, I see." She laughed. "He must not know what you're like when you've had some wine."

"Hey, you're not one to talk." Suzie grinned.

"You are so right. Anyway, at least the wedding plans are getting finalized."

"Now, we just have to make sure that the bride and groom attend the wedding."

"I don't think that will be an issue. I'm going to put dinner on," Mary said. "Is pasta okay?"

"Perfect, I'll get a bottle of wine."

Suzie and Mary spent the rest of the night talking about Mary's failed marriage and how their lives had changed so much since they had moved to Dune House.

Chapter Four

"Morning Mary," Suzie said as she came downstairs for breakfast the following morning.

"Morning." Mary already had coffee and eggs ready on the table.

"Thank you," Suzie said as she sat down in front of her plate.

"I heard the shower," Mary said. "So I got breakfast ready."

"I just spoke to Paul. He's going to hang around the docks and see if he hears anything, and I'm going to work on the centerpieces and then head out to pick him up after lunch. Summer should know more about the murder then."

"Sounds like a plan."

"Hopefully there's something about the murder that she is prepared to tell us."

Suzie spent the rest of the morning working on the centerpieces. She had always loved decorating and found the process relaxing even though the murder often entered her thoughts.

"I'm going to see Summer now, Mary," Suzie said as she walked into the kitchen. "Is there anything that you need from town?"

"No, I think we're okay here. Don't you want lunch first?"

"No thank you, I'm not very hungry."

"Okay, tell Summer I said hi, and here." She handed her a list. "Let her go over these details and make sure that they are what she wanted. I added a few of my own ideas and I don't want her to think I'm taking over."

"That's very kind of you, Mary. I'll show her a picture of the centerpieces, too. I'm not sure if she will like them."

Mary looked over at the table where Suzie had worked on the centerpieces and gasped. "Suzie, they're beautiful. She's going to love them. They look just like a little beach." The square centerpieces had sand and paper that was shaped and decorated to look like crashing waves.

"It wasn't exactly what Summer wanted, but I thought it might go along with her nautical theme. But, do you think it's too over the top?"

"No, I don't think so at all."

"I guess all that matters is what Summer thinks." Suzie smiled as she snapped a picture of the centerpieces. "Call me if you need anything."

As Suzie left Dune House she sent a text to Paul that she was going to visit Summer. He texted back right away that he would be ready when she arrived. As he said he would be, he was waiting for her when she pulled up. She looked over at the police cars that were present. They still swarmed the docks, but they had thinned out a lot from yesterday. When she looked at Paul he looked like he hadn't slept. His eyes had dark rings around them, but he looked determined.

"How are you?" Suzie asked.

"I'm fine." He smiled at her. "Everyone is so tight lipped about the murder."

"Maybe they'll be more talkative once the police disappear." Suzie started to drive towards the medical examiner's office. When she arrived she noticed that there were no other cars in the parking lot, aside from Summer's. Inside the main reception room Summer was nowhere to be seen.

"Dr. Rose?" Suzie called out, but Summer did not respond.

"She's probably in the back." Suzie followed the faint sound of music. Just as she started to push the door open she froze. "You should let me handle this part."

"It will be fine."

Suzie pushed the door open slightly, but just before she called out Summer's name she stopped, she could overhear Summer speaking to someone. Suzie stood with the door slightly open and listened.

"It was something short and sharp. Not a knife. That's all I know right now. I'm checking into different weapons that might have caused the wound, but haven't found anything definitive." Suzie looked at Paul with wide eyes. There was no other voice that they could hear so Suzie presumed that Summer was on the phone. "There were no defensive wounds, but the strike did come from the front." After a short pause she continued. "Okay, I'll send over the report now." Suzie presumed that Summer had hung up. Suzie waited a few seconds before she said anything. She didn't want Summer to suspect that they might have been eavesdropping. Summer turned on some soft music.

"Dr. Rose?" Suzie called out.

"Suzie, I'll be right out." Summer turned off the music. "I'm sorry, Paul, it helps me to concentrate," she said as she walked out of the back room.

"That's okay, you have nothing to apologize

for," Paul said.

"Did you find out anything?" Suzie asked as they walked towards the front.

"You know I can't tell you anything. Jason asked me to keep it pinned up tight."

"But..." Paul started to object.

"It's okay, Paul." Suzie held his hand gently and looked at Summer. "I wanted to tell you that everything is coming together with organizing the wedding." Suzie smiled trying to break the tension. "Here is a list from Mary in case there's anything you want to change and a picture of the centerpieces." Suzie showed Summer her cell phone. "They're a bit different from what you wanted, so be honest if you like them."

"Thank you, Suzie," Summer said. "These are gorgeous."

"Sorry Summer," Paul said. "I didn't mean to put you in an awkward position. I just need to know who did this."

"I understand." Summer smiled slightly. "We'll get to the bottom of it. I know this must be difficult for you."

"I'm fine really. The only difficult thing is not knowing who did this." He shoved his hands into his pockets. "Once that's settled, I'll be fine."

Suzie and Summer exchanged a quick glance of concern, but Suzie didn't argue the point.

"I'll go through the list and get back to Mary."

"Okay, let me know if you need anything." Suzie smiled.

As Suzie and Paul left the medical examiner's office Paul turned to Suzie. "Let's go over what we know."

"Well, from the phone call we know that the weapon was short and sharp and that he didn't have any defensive wounds, so he was probably surprised by the killer."

"Given that, he most likely knew the person," Paul said thoughtfully.

"Not to mention that there was no sign of forced entry."

"Yes, but fishermen often don't lock their cabins."

"That's true," Suzie said. "But given the fact that he was attacked from the front and there were no defensive wounds it makes it seem as if it was someone that he wouldn't expect an attack from."

"We need to find out who that is. There is no time to waste." Paul turned and walked towards the car. Suzie stared at him for a moment. It was clear that he wouldn't stop until he found the murderer. Once in the car again, Paul pointed to the docks. "Can you drop me off at my boat?"

"Sure, but are you certain you don't want to sleep at Dune House?"

"No, I'm going to sleep on the boat again tonight," Paul said. "I want to see if I can find out anything. See if they'll talk now that there aren't so many police milling around." Suzie nodded as they drove towards the docks. She knew that she wouldn't be able to change his mind.

She pulled to a stop in front of the docks and looked over at him. "Let me stay with you."

"No, that's not a good idea."

"You need to stop worrying so much about protecting me."

"You first." He held her gaze. His lips curled into a slow smile.

"I see your point." Suzie sighed and leaned over to kiss him.

"I'll see you first thing in the morning?"

"Yes. We can also talk to some of the fishermen in the morning who don't sleep on their boats and see if anyone knows anything."

She kissed his cheek just before he climbed out of the car. Suzie looked at him as he walked off. He needed his space and she needed time to try and work out anything more she could about the murder.

Chapter Five

Back at Dune House Suzie could barely get her feet on the ground before Mary rushed up to her.

"How did it go with Summer?"

"She didn't tell us anything, but we did overhear a few things about the murder."

"But, how is she?" Mary searched her eyes.

"Oh, she seems okay." Suzie frowned. "Troubled by all of this of course, and concerned about the wedding."

"Poor girl." Mary clucked her tongue.

"Summer's strong. She'll be okay. She said that she would call you about the wedding later." Suzie followed Mary into Dune House and glanced at the papers on the table. "Plans?"

"Yes, I'm still working on them. Things are a bit calmer though. What do you think about doves?"

"Real doves?"

"Yes, just a few live ones to fly out at the end of the ceremony?"

"I think it's a little much, Mary." Suzie sat down at the kitchen table and closed her eyes. "I think it might be better to keep things as simple as possible right now. It's not looking too promising that this case is going to be solved quickly and it would be a shame for the unsolved murder to be hanging over their heads during the wedding."

"Oh." Mary nodded as she sat down beside her. "I understand." She rubbed Suzie's shoulder. "Try not to worry too much, Suzie. No matter what, the crime will be solved, and Summer and Jason will be married. How it happens, when it happens, is not as big of a deal as we might think it is."

"Thanks Mary." Suzie smiled slightly. "To be honest I'm a little concerned about Paul. I'm not so accustomed to being wrapped up in the feelings of another person."

"You get more wrapped up than you realize, Suzie. Do you remember my wedding?"

Suzie grinned and tapped her fingers on the table. "A toast to the man I will murder if he breaks my best friend's heart."

"Yes, it was the talk of the reception." Mary laughed.

"I'm sorry I didn't follow through with it." Suzie shook her head.

"You did much better than that. You created this home for us, where we both get to be ourselves."

"We created it together." Suzie held her gaze. "Dune House wouldn't be here without you, Mary. Just like Summer and Jason wouldn't get to have such a lovely wedding if it wasn't for you."

"I can't help it. I'm still a romantic at heart." She winked at Suzie.

"Speaking of romance. What's going on with

your detective?"

"Oh, he's out of town. I'm sure that I'll be hearing from him this evening."

"I'm so glad things are working out."

"Yes, we're just taking it slow. No need to rush."

"True. Do you want to go for a walk?" Suzie asked.

"Yes, I could use some fresh air."

Suzie and Mary walked along the beach in a comfortable silence. Suzie's mind did not stop going over the facts of the case. By the time they had returned to Dune House the sun was beginning to set.

"I'm going to try to turn in early," Suzie said once they were inside. "I am going to the docks to meet Paul first thing in the morning so we can ask around and see if anyone knows anything about the murder."

"No dinner?" Mary clucked her tongue.

"That's no way to keep your strength up."

"I know, but I'm not very hungry. Maybe I'll get up in a little while to eat."

"Okay, there's roast in the refrigerator if you want it."

"I'm sure I'll dig into it at some point. Thanks Mary." She hugged her friend then headed off to her room. As she settled into sleep her mind raced with thoughts of the case. When they finally slowed down and she was able to fall asleep, her dreams filled with rough, rogue waves that threatened the docks and Dune House.

Suzie woke in the morning to the scent of oatmeal. The cinnamon called to her. After a quick shower she threw on some clothes and headed out into the kitchen. Much to her surprise she found Paul already there.

"Morning." He smiled at her. "I thought I'd meet you here because I wanted a walk."

"You didn't sleep, did you?"

"I did a little. Not much."

"I must have gotten all of your sleep for you. I'm starving. Thanks so much, Mary." Mary set a bowl of oatmeal down in front of her.

"No problem."

"We all have some work ahead of us today," Suzie said.

"Yes." Paul wiped a hand across his face. "I just hope that it pays off."

"We'll find something." Suzie smiled at him. "Let me text Jason and see if he has any updates."

"Do you think he will answer?" Paul asked.

"He might."

"I don't know." Paul swirled a spoon through his oatmeal. "Maybe we should just leave him out of it. I don't think he'll be very forthcoming with information. If he had information for us, he would have contacted us, don't you think?"

"You're right. He'll contact us when he wants to." Suzie nodded.

"Wait a minute." Mary frowned. "What about the wedding? If Jason and Summer are working on the investigation, then how are they going to have time to finish the preparations?"

"If you continue helping them the way you are they'll be fine," Suzie said. "I don't think Jason's going to mind a little helping hand with the investigation."

"I think he might." Mary shrugged. "But he's your cousin and he probably already knows that you won't stay out of it. You can see what you can find out and I'll continue to help Summer."

"You're right, he might mind it a little, but once the dust settles he'll understand. Besides, we're not going to cause any trouble, we're just going to help."

"Your version of help isn't always trouble-free." Mary raised an eyebrow and hid her face behind her mug of coffee.

"I know, I know." Suzie glanced over at Paul. "But we have to try."

"Absolutely," Paul said.

Suzie finished the last few spoons of her oatmeal, then turned to Paul. "Ready?"

"Yes." He nodded.

"Remember Paul, we're just going to have some friendly conversations. We don't want to do anything to spook anyone."

"I'll behave." He smiled a little. "At least I intend to."

"Thanks again, Mary." Suzie led Paul out through the door. She opened the car doors with a button on her keyring. Paul climbed in, and she followed after him. When she started the ignition, music blasted through the speakers.

"What is that?" He winced and turned the radio down.

"Oh sorry, I must have been listening to a good song." She laughed. "Sometimes I like to drive around with the window rolled down and music blasting."

"I can appreciate that." He smiled at her and turned the volume up enough to enjoy the current song. "I wasn't able to get any information on the docks last night. There weren't many people around."

When they arrived at the docks the parking lot was devoid of any police cars. Suzie felt a sense of relief, but also a good amount of irritation. She didn't want to be shooed away by officers, but she also wondered why they weren't there conducting an investigation.

"I guess the police are done with the crime scene." She frowned.

"Which is exactly why we need to pick up where they left off." He stretched his arms and yawned. "Where should we start?"

"I think the best place to start is canvasing the dock for anyone that might have seen something. I know the police already did, but we might still be able to find out some information."

"Some of the captains aren't too friendly with

the police, they're not likely to give up any real information."

"Even to Jason?"

"Yes, even Jason. Police is police."

"I didn't realize there was so much tension."

"It's not as bad as you might think, but since the main suspects are going to be people on the docks, they are going to get defensive about any questions the police ask. They're going to get defensive about anything that I ask, too."

"Maybe I should do the talking then."

"Definitely not. In fact it might be better if you wait at the car."

"But you know there's no chance of that happening." She smiled sweetly at him. He stared into her eyes for a moment.

"If I..."

"Nope."

"Suzie, I think..."

"It's not going to happen. I'm going to be by your side the entire time." She reached out and patted his cheek. "I'm looking forward to meeting your friends, darling."

"I think you'll change your mind once you've met them." He chuckled. "All right, let's go."

When she walked towards the docks she was startled by how quiet they were. Usually there were fishermen, and locals milling about. "If anyone is even out here to question."

"They're here, they're just hiding out. Because of that." He pointed to the police tape wrapped around Robbie's boat.

"I never realized fishermen were such an unruly bunch." Suzie raised an eyebrow.

"They aren't always. But marrying the sea, it makes a man a bit rough around the edges."

"Does that make me your mistress?" She winked at him.

"Never." He held her gaze. "I've kept my

options open, never made a full commitment."

"Oh, I see." She laughed and slipped her arm through his. As they stepped onto the dock, she noticed a man towards the end of it. The moment he saw them, he bolted towards one of the boats. "There." Suzie pointed in the man's direction. "I bet he knows something."

"Let's catch up with him." Paul quickened his pace.

"I think he went on this boat." Suzie walked towards the boat and spotted the man as he disappeared inside the cabin. She glanced back at Paul who nodded at her. Suzie mounted the boat, side stepped a container of empty oyster shells, and walked over to the cabin door with Paul right behind her. She knocked twice then stepped back. The man inside the cabin opened the door and snarled at her.

"What is it?"

"Careful how you talk to a lady." Paul raised a bushy eyebrow and stepped in front of Suzie.

"Pedro, we just have a couple of questions for you."

"I bet, you and the entire police department."

"No, just us." Suzie smiled at him. "You know Paul don't you?" She gestured to Paul.

"Sure, I know him. That doesn't mean I'm going to say anything."

"I'm not here to give you a hard time." Paul rested one hand on the door frame of the cabin. "All we want to know is whether you saw anyone around Robbie's boat. He was one of us and I'd like to get to the bottom of his murder. You can't blame me for that, can you?"

"No, I can't, but you know what happens once you get involved with the cops. They just like to dig into things that are none of their business. I'm not sure how you can expect me to expose myself to that."

"No need to." Suzie shook her head. "All we want to do is get some information. That information is going to stay between you and us, it will have nothing to do with the police."

"Not even your cousin, Jason?" He raised an eyebrow. "Yes, I know who you are."

"Pedro, relax. Just because her cousin is a cop, that doesn't make her one, now does it?"

"You tell me." Pedro crossed his arms and stared at both of them. Suzie noticed that he had a bandage around his right hand. She knew from experience with Paul that minor injuries often occurred at sea and it reminded her what a tough job fisherman had.

"I just want to find out what happened to Robbie as I'm sure you do," Suzie said.

"How do I know this whole conversation isn't being recorded?"

"All I want to know is whether you saw anyone." Suzie shrugged. "How could that be used against you?"

"I'm sure that they could come up with a way."

"So?" Paul leaned closer to him. "Did you see anything or not?"

"Since you were friends with Robbie, I guess I should tell you." He drew a deep breath and then sighed. "I saw a guy. I didn't know who he was. But he wore this bright yellow jacket so it was hard to miss him. He seemed to be snooping around Robbie's boat." He gestured towards the boat. "You know, we try to look out for each other around here, so I was going to say something to him, but by the time I got off my boat he was gone."

"Did you see where he went? Did he go to the parking lot?"

"No, not that I saw. He was just gone. I figured I must have missed him leaving the dock somehow. Anyway, that's all I know."

"The man in the bright yellow jacket, was he tall? Thin?" Suzie narrowed her eyes.

"No, just about average." He squinted. "I don't pay much attention to that. I did notice that he was bald. Not a hair on his head."

"I understand. Thank you for your help." Suzie nodded at him.

"Just do me a favor and forget my name when you talk to your cousin about this."

"I wouldn't dream of mentioning it." She smiled. "But I will remember it, because you did a good thing by telling us what you know."

"Sure, if you say so." He shrugged. "Now, if you don't mind, I have work to do."

"What did you do to your hand?" Suzie asked.

"I work as a fisherman. What do you think I did to it? I cut it." He scowled.

"What about Robbie? Did you notice anything strange about him lately?" Suzie asked.

"Like what?"

"Like, anything he might have been involved in that would have led to this," Suzie said.

"Paul, you know we stay out of each others'

business." Pedro turned towards Paul and stared hard at him.

"Right, but one of us ended up murdered, I think it's okay to ask a few questions," Paul said.

"Maybe you do, but the rest of us don't. If Robbie was into something it was his business, and I'm not going to talk about it."

"So, he was into something?" Paul's tone hardened.

"You would have known about that, wouldn't you, Paul? I mean you were friends."

"He never said anything to me."

"Because it wasn't your business."

Suzie reached up and touched Paul's arm as she noticed his muscles twitch.

"It is now." He scowled. "If anyone has a problem with that, they can say it to my face."

"All right, all right." Pedro held up his hands. "I'm just reminding you of how things work around here."

"Maybe you're the one that needs reminding, of how we take care of our own."

"Ouch." He rolled his eyes.

"If you think of anything else." Suzie offered him a card for Dune House. "I can be reached here."

"Sure, thanks." He nodded at her then turned away. Once they were off the boat, Paul spun on his heel and looked straight at her.

"Do you see what I mean now?"

"Yes, I do, but it's nothing I haven't run into before, Paul. But I noticed you got a little riled up."

"He just got under my skin."

"I noticed."

"Here, let's talk to Frank, he might have seen something. He lives on his boat and only goes out for short runs."

Suzie let the subject drop. As she trailed after him, she noticed a few faces peering through

63

windows on their boats. She gritted her teeth and caught up to Paul.

"Frank." He clapped a hand on the rail of the man's boat. Frank turned to look at him. He was big, thicker than Paul and taller, too.

"Hey Paul." He nodded. "What do you need?"

"I just wanted to know if you saw anything strange around the dock in the past few days."

"You mean about Robbie?" Frank stared hard at the rope he coiled around his arm.

"Yes." Paul leaned closer to him. "Did you notice anything?"

"Only you here, asking me questions." Frank met his eyes. "That's pretty strange."

"Don't start the 'what happens on the dock stays on the dock' business with me. Robbie deserved better than that."

Frank nodded slowly and returned to his coiling. "You may be right about that. I personally kept my distance. I saw him come in and out of here too many times to believe he was just catching shellfish."

"What do you mean by that?" Paul narrowed his eyes.

"I don't mean anything. I just said, it's not my concern."

"What was he into?" Paul swung his foot over the side of the boat and climbed on.

"Back off, I have nothing to say."

"Was it drugs or something? Was he running drugs?"

"I can't say, I don't know." Frank shrugged. "It's not like I inspected his boat. All I know is that the way he kept moving in and out at odd hours was suspicious."

"Frank, I'm not trying to drag Robbie through the mud, I just want to find out who did this."

"Why are you asking questions about that?"

"Because Robbie was my friend, no matter what he was into."

"No, I mean, why are you asking questions, Paul?" He looked at Paul. "I think we both know who did this."

"We do?" Paul raised an eyebrow. "Please, enlighten me."

"Look whose boat is right next to Robbie's." He pointed down the stretch of dock. Paul turned his attention in the direction that he pointed.

"Is that Mike's?" He squinted.

"Sure is."

"So?" Paul looked back at him.

"You didn't hear?"

"No." Paul shook his head. "Were Robbie and Mike having problems?"

"Is there anyone that Mike didn't have problems with? You really can't tell me that you don't think that Mike didn't have something to do with this."

"All I can tell you is that I don't know for sure who did. But now that you pointed out whose boat was docked beside Robbie's, I will be having a conversation with Mike. Anything else you can tell us about that day? Anyone suspicious?"

"What about someone in a yellow jacket?" Suzie stepped closer to the boat.

"A yellow jacket?" Frank looked over at the parking lot. "I don't think so. I mean, a few people wear them around here, but most of the fishermen wear orange jackets. It's good for visibility. Nothing stood out to me."

"No one sneaking around Robbie's boat?" Paul stepped back off Frank's boat.

"Like I said, the moment things started getting shady, I stopped paying attention. Better not to know, than to pretend not to know. You know?"

"I hear you." Paul nodded.

Suzie handed Frank one of her cards. "If you think of anything, maybe you don't feel comfortable going to the police about, just give me a call here."

"Okay." He tucked the business card into the side pocket of his shirt. "Good luck. Be careful with Mike." He met Suzie's eyes.

"I will be." She smiled.

Chapter Six

As Suzie fell into step beside Paul, he seemed to slow down.

"I don't know if this is such a good idea. Maybe we should let Jason speak to him."

"Paul? Are you feeling okay?" She reached up and touched his forehead lightly with her fingertips. "I've never heard you talk like this before."

"I get the point, but seriously, Mike isn't the easiest guy to get along with. The only person he talks nicely to is his wife. I don't want you to get into any danger. It might be better to have Jason here as back-up, instead of just barging onto his boat."

"I don't intend to barge onto his boat, but we also don't have time to wait for Jason to show up and if he does I don't think he'll be very happy that we are talking to people about the murder. I think we should have a quick conversation with the guy at least. How bad could he be?"

"If you say so." He nodded to Suzie. "You're the one in charge here."

"I wouldn't say that."

"You've heard my opinion, I don't think we should go over there without back-up. Now it's up to you to decide what we do."

"I think it's worth at least trying to talk to the man. He is the one who is most likely to have a view of the murder, also, he could be the killer himself. Either way we need to speak to this man."

"All right." He shook his head. "But my protest is on record."

"Noted." Suzie nodded. She approached Mike's boat. Luckily he was outside on the deck. She watched for a moment as he polished the railing of his boat. His methodical movements didn't make him seem like a particularly wild man.

"Excuse me, Mike?" She smiled as sweet as she could. He didn't respond. Paul frowned.

"Mike, we just want to talk to you for a minute," Paul said.

Still Mike swept the cloth along the railing and didn't even bother to look up at them. Paul gritted his teeth and climbed onto the boat.

"Mike. Did you hear me?"

"Get off my boat." He rubbed the cloth over the railing with sharper, forceful movements. "I didn't invite you on here. I could have you arrested for being here."

Suzie stepped onto the boat as well and stood beside Paul.

"Relax Mike, we just have a few questions for you." Paul tried to meet the man's eyes. He looked over at Suzie and shook his head.

"I'm not answering any more questions. It's pretty clear to me why you're here, and no I didn't have anything to do with Robbie's death. Not that you will believe me. So get off my boat." He finally looked up. His gaze skipped from Paul's face, to Suzie's.

"You too."

"We're not going anywhere until we get some information from you." Suzie folded her arms across her chest.

"Suzie, we shouldn't antagonize the situation." Paul put his hand lightly on one of her elbows. "Let's just go."

"No." Suzie placed her feet hard on the floor. "I'm not moving. I want to know what he knows, even if I have to stand here all day. Do you have a problem with that, Paul?"

"No, of course not." Paul straightened up beside her. "I'm here with you."

"Oh, how great. Let me just call the police. Oh, that's right, I can't, because your old lady here has family on the police force. Doesn't she?" He glared at Suzie. Suzie bit back a comment about how rude he was being.

"Jason has nothing to do with us being here. We're here because we were told you likely had the best idea of what happened to Robbie," Suzie said.

"Right. I can tell you that he was a pain in my behind. Is that what you want to hear?"

"No, that's not what we're looking for. I would think you'd be a little more concerned about a murder that took place right next door."

"I have a lot on my mind." He shoved his cabin door open. Suzie noticed a pile of crumpled laundry and an extra blanket on the cot inside. If he was docked, why hadn't he taken his laundry home yet? Paul said that he was married so surely he didn't live on the boat.

"Mike, seriously. Just answer the question." Paul took an intimidating step forward. Suzie watched as his shoulders straightened and his chest spread. He squinted at Mike. He meant business. Mike glared right back at him with no sign of backing down.

"I don't have to answer your questions, Paul. You are nothing but a fisherman, or have you forgotten that?"

"I haven't forgotten who I am, but I'm starting to wonder if you have forgotten who you are. We're a brotherhood, we're supposed to stick together. You're really going to let someone come on these docks and commit murder?"

"A brotherhood?" Mike laughed and shook his head. "You really are ancient aren't you, Paul? There's no brotherhood here, at least not one that I'm a part of. You're going to need to drop that nonsense and get off my boat."

"I'm not going anywhere." Paul spread his feet shoulder width apart and sank his weight into his heels. Suzie sensed a confrontation building.

"Okay, we'll go." She put a hand on Paul's arm. His muscles tensed beneath her touch. "I'm sure there are plenty of other people we can ask about the man in the yellow jacket, and of course, about your whereabouts since you are so uncooperative."

"What did you just say to me?" His words were rough as he stepped towards her. Paul moved between them before Mike could get anywhere near her.

"I said, if you want to make yourself look like a suspect go right ahead. It's usually the people who have something to hide that don't want to answer questions," Suzie said.

"You have no right to talk to me like that. Get off my boat before I call the real cops and cause a scene. Is that what you want?"

"No." Paul's eyes locked to his. "I thought you might want to solve the murder of a fellow fisherman, but I guess all of the rumors about you are true."

"People can say whatever they want. I don't care. My life is not going to change based on what anyone thinks of me. You want to point a finger at me? Go right ahead. I have nothing to hide." He pulled his phone out of his pocket. "But if you don't move off my boat in the next five seconds I will be placing that call. Or if you prefer I could just toss your lady friend here into the drink. Hm?"

Suzie glared at him and was about to step forward to defend herself, but Paul remained in front of her and spoke first.

"Watch it Mike, I draw the line when it comes to threatening a woman," Paul said.

"Go ahead and draw it. Your line doesn't mean anything to me." He pushed a button on the phone.

"Let's just go, Paul. It's not worth it." Suzie tugged at his arm.

"Fine." He nodded and followed after her as she stepped off the boat. Once they were both on the dock, Paul looked over at her with a heavy stare. "Mike's a rough character."

"He might be, but he's also a possible suspect.

I couldn't walk away without at least trying to get some information out of him."

"You shouldn't have." He glanced over his shoulder at Mike's boat. "He's the type to hold a grudge."

"I'm not sure what it is about me that gives you the impression that there is anything delicate about me, but I can assure you I have handled many Mikes in my life, and he's not even the worst."

"And my point is, you shouldn't have to do that anymore." He wrapped his arm around her shoulders. "You have me now. So, let me do my job, hm?"

"Your job?" She would have protested if she could have stopped smiling. "I like the sound of that."

"Get used to it." He winked at her.

Chapter Seven

When Suzie and Paul reached the car Suzie paused and pulled out her phone.

"I think we need to get in contact with Jason."

"From what Summer said yesterday I don't think he's going to want to tell us much about the investigation. And the way he spoke to me after we had found Robbie." Paul raised an eyebrow. "It was only out of respect for you that I held my tongue."

"I know that, and I appreciate that. Jason is just wound up about getting this investigation completed and done correctly so that there are no bumps in the road when it comes to closing the case. You can understand that, can't you?"

"Of course I can. But there's only so much I'll take. Jason already knows that."

"Paul, don't forget, I'm the only family he's got. He has no one to stand with him at the wedding." She bit into her bottom lip then looked over at him again. "In fact, I was wondering if you might like to be one of his groomsmen."

"Isn't it a little late for that?" Paul frowned.

"I don't think so."

"I'm pretty sure he's supposed to ask." He laughed. "Maybe you should check with him first."

"Jason's too proud to ask anything of anyone."

"Well, I prefer to wait and see if he asks me himself."

"I understand," Suzie agreed. "I'll see what I can get out of him about the investigation. Maybe if we talk to him in a gentle way, he'll be willing to share information with us?"

"All right, but I think you're the better candidate to be gentle. Hm?"

"I suppose I am." She pulled out her cell phone and dialed Jason's number. After the fourth ring she was about to give up.

"What is it Suzie?"

She was startled by the bite in his voice. "Jason, I'm just calling to see if there are any new developments in Robbie's case."

"The case that you've been looking into behind my back?"

"Jason?"

"Suzie?"

She gripped the phone tight and looked over at Paul before she turned away and lowered her voice. "This was a friend of Paul's we just want to find out the truth."

"Maybe so, but you should have left this to me and kept out of it."

"Well, I couldn't let it go. Can we meet and share information?"

"You think you have information to share with me?"

"Yes, I think so."

"All right. Meet me at Dune House in fifteen minutes. I can only spare a few minutes."

"Thanks Jason."

"Just remember, Suzie, you need to stay out of this from now on. Having a witness call me and complain that you have been interrogating them is a problem."

"Who called to complain?"

"Never mind that. I'll see you at Dune House."

Suzie hung up the phone and turned back to Paul. "He wants to meet with us at Dune House."

"And?" He studied her. "There's something more to it than that isn't there?"

"No, I think he's just a little uptight. He said that someone called to complain about us asking questions at the docks."

"That was fast." Paul looked over his shoulder and squinted at the boats. "I'm going to guess it was Mike."

"Yes, you're probably right."

"But if it was him then I doubt he was the murderer. Why would he want to draw attention to himself?"

"He might think that if he is open with the police they won't suspect him. Or he's so cocky he doesn't think he'll be caught," Suzie suggested. "I've seen it before."

Suzie and Paul climbed back into the car and headed back to Dune House. When they arrived Mary greeted them at the door.

"Jason is on his way to talk to me and Paul." Suzie gestured to the large kitchen table. "We'll use this space if that's okay."

"Sure, it's fine. Any news?"

"Not exactly." Suzie frowned. "Maybe a suspect, but not enough to go on just yet."

"Okay, I'm going to head upstairs to finish cleaning." As Mary left Suzie saw Jason in the entrance of the kitchen. "Hi Jason."

"Hi." Jason smiled. "Sorry, I don't have long.

What did you find out?" He looked straight at Paul.

"Suzie?" Paul glanced over at her.

"We spoke to a few people on the docks who mentioned seeing a man wearing a bright yellow jacket and one of the fisherman in particular gave us reason to believe he might himself be the murderer."

"Mike?" Jason raised an eyebrow.

"Yes." Suzie's eyes widened. "You came to the same conclusion?"

"Yes. He's not exactly the friendly type, but there's more to it than that. Apparently he lodged a complaint with the dock owner. He was bothered by Robbie coming in and out at all hours. That gives him a motive."

"A little too much noise is a reason to kill someone?" Suzie shook her head. "That seems like a stretch."

"You met Mike, right?" Jason raised an

eyebrow. "Seems to me that guy has a short fuse."

"Maybe. Or maybe he's just extra stressed about something." Suzie narrowed her eyes. "He's married?"

Jason glanced down at his phone. "Yes."

"But he's staying on his boat." She tapped her chin. "Sounds like they're having problems. Maybe that's why he's so cranky."

"Maybe," Jason said.

"I'll make a note to talk to his wife." Suzie took her cell phone out of her pocket.

"You'll do no such thing," Jason said. "You don't want to make a bad situation worse."

"I'm sure a friendly conversation won't do any harm."

"Suzie, I know my protests fall on deaf ears when it comes to stuff like this, but you need to listen to me. You cannot interfere in this investigation."

"Okay." Suzie put her phone away. She knew

84

that there was no reason to argue with Jason about it as she would be fighting a losing battle.

"Haven't you been able to find anything else out?" Paul's brows knitted together.

"I'm doing my best." He locked eyes with Paul. "I did find out his recent routes. His boat has a GPS tracker."

"And? Anything from them?"

"I was hoping you could tell me. It seems that some of the destinations are a bit odd for fishing. Would you look them over for me?"

"Sure." Paul took the piece of paper from Jason and began to look it over.

"I still think we need to find out who the man in the bright yellow jacket was," Suzie said. "If he wasn't the killer, then maybe he's a witness. We need to pinpoint who it was."

"I agree, but it's hard to find someone based on just that." Jason rubbed his chin. "Without a little more information I'm afraid we're not going to get very far."

"The witness mentioned that he was bald," Suzie said.

"Still not a lot to go on." Jason shrugged.

"This can't be right." Paul glanced up at him. "Did you get the right route information?"

"It came right off the boat's GPS tracker. We matched the coordinates to these locations." Jason squinted at the paper. "Do you see something unusual?"

"Just about all of it is unusual. There's no reason that he should have gone to some of these places. Are you certain that you got the right information?" He studied Jason.

"Yes Paul, I'm certain." Jason's tone grew short. "I know how to download route information from a GPS tracker. Why are these locations unusual?"

"It's not that the locations are unusual it's just that there's no reason for Robbie to go to some of them. Some of them are residential and one is in the middle of nowhere. There just isn't a reason for him to waste fuel traveling to some of these places. The places to fish for shellfish are much closer."

"Well, that's what was on the GPS."

"Maybe he had other business?" Suzie glanced between the two men. "Could he have been there for different reasons?"

Paul opened his mouth as if he might have something to say, but closed it again.

"Paul? Do you know anything about the locations?" Jason folded his arms across his chest.

"No. Not really. Nothing more than you would."

"Well, then I guess we are at a standstill. The most I can do is hope that surveillance cameras caught an image of the bright yellow jacket man as he left the docks. If we can get a face we might be able to get a name."

"Let me know if you find anything, please?" Suzie said.

"I'll tell you what I can," Jason said sternly.

"Thank you." Suzie smiled.

"Do you want to keep that? It's a copy." Jason pointed to the paper in Paul's hands. "That way if you think of anything you can let me know."

"Okay. Thanks Jason." He cleared his throat. "You doing okay?"

Jason glanced over at him. "Huh?"

"Well I mean, if you have any uh, anything you need help with for the wedding."

"Mary's taking care of it," Jason said.

Suzie hid a smile as Paul rubbed the back of his neck. "I know that, Jason, but if you need any, you know advice."

"What?" Jason's eyes widened. "Oh, no thanks, Paul, I think I can handle that."

"That's not what I meant!" Paul groaned.

"I think Paul is just offering you an ear if you need it. You're surrounded by women, Jason, sometimes it's nice to get a male perspective."

Jason chuckled. "All right, that was a good laugh. I needed it. Thanks Paul." He clapped him on the shoulder. In that moment all of the tension between them relaxed. Suzie gave Jason a quick hug.

"Just let us know if you need help with anything."

"I will." He started to turn away, then hesitated and turned back. "Actually, I do have a problem I could use your help with, Paul."

"What's that?" Paul smiled.

"One of my buddies from school isn't going to be able to make the wedding. So, I have a spot for a groomsman I need to fill. I was just going to let it go, but I know it'll throw off the balance. I mean, I know it means putting on a suit, but if..."

"I'll do it." Paul nodded. "I'll get fitted as soon

as I can."

"Great. Thanks." Jason smiled. "All right, I'm going to see if I can find out any more information about the murder weapon. Let me know if you two come up with anything."

"We will." Suzie walked him to the door. Once he was gone she turned and walked back to Paul. "You are going to look so handsome in a suit."

"Ha, don't get used to it." He grinned.

"A suit," Mary said as she entered the kitchen.

"Jason asked Paul to be a groomsman."

"Oh good, finally." Mary walked over to a stack of papers. "Here's the number for the tailor." She handed him a slip of paper.

"I'll check on it as soon as I can. Suzie, I'm going to head back to the boat. I have a few things I need to take care of, okay?"

"Sure, let me know if I can help with anything. I'm sure Mary could use a hand with some of this wedding stuff."

"I have to admit, I'm worn out." Mary shook her head. "I forgot just how much work planning a wedding is."

"Great. I'll see you in the morning then, Suzie. We'll head out first thing, all right?"

"Yes." Suzie walked him to the door and kissed him goodbye. Once she and Mary were alone she turned back to her with a heavy sigh.

"What chaos!"

"I agree." Mary laughed. "You should see the list of things I need to change for the wedding. It turns out that even though Summer said she didn't mind about some things she has a definite opinion about what she wants."

"How do we get ourselves into these messes?" Suzie plopped down on the couch. Mary sat down beside her.

"Because, we like to help people."

"Right, right, but why?" Suzie yawned.

"That I haven't found an explanation for. Let

me get you something to eat."

"I can get it. You take a break, Mary. Then we'll go over what we can do about these wedding issues."

Suzie's mind swirled from thoughts of suits to thoughts of murder. As she tried to put every piece together and into its proper place she stood up and walked into the kitchen. Maybe there was a lot to deal with, but it was a far cry from the quiet life she'd fallen into before she ended up at Dune House. There was some beauty to the chaos that being close to loved ones could create.

Chapter Eight

After straightening out some wedding details with Mary, Suzie called it a night and crawled into bed. She thought for sure that she would fall right to sleep. Instead she tossed and turned. Her mind filled with what they might find the next day, and also what Summer and Jason's wedding would be like. With so much to keep her awake, she could barely keep her eyes closed. After a few hours of trying to convince herself to rest, her eyes popped open yet again.

The sliver of moonlight that made its way through the curtains to slice across her bedroom floor was to blame. At least that's what she told herself as she climbed out of bed and walked towards the window. She pulled the curtains tight and walked back to her bed. When she closed her eyes again she was sure she would fall asleep. However, a few minutes later her eyes sprang open once more. Her heart fluttered with the weight of her frustration. How could she waste time laying in bed?

Driven to her feet she grabbed some clothes to change into. As she dressed she experienced a sensation of determination. She wanted to go to the docks and have a look around. She wanted to see if there was anything they had missed. Suzie slipped out of her room and grabbed her keys on her way through the kitchen. As quietly as she could she let herself out through the front door. Without hesitation she drove to the docks and parked.

Right away she noticed that Paul's boat was in darkness. He was probably sound asleep. Still, it made her feel a little more secure just to know that he was there. She walked along the edge of the dock in the hopes that she wouldn't disturb anyone. Truly, she had no idea what she was searching for. Maybe a scrap of paper? A drop of blood? Neither would be hard to find on a very populated dock.

It occurred to her that perhaps the killer disposed of the murder weapon in one of the trashcans. She stopped at the first one and lifted the lid. The smell hit her like a wave and knocked her back with just as much force. A combination of rotten fish, old gym socks, and whatever scraps of food the fishermen didn't eat, made her nostrils burn with disgust. Still, she took a deep breath, and poked her head back over the top of the trashcan. It was only half full and too slimy to dig through. She put the lid back on it, and walked towards the next trashcan. When she lifted the lid she saw that this trashcan was full to the brim. The papers that covered the top were fairly clean so she dug through them to see what was underneath. The trash shifted with her movement, but she found nothing. She sighed. She had hoped to find something, but even if there had been something to find surely the bins had been searched by the police since the murder.

Suzie walked further along the dock. She looked down at the wooden boards in despair. She walked past Robbie's boat which still had the crime scene tape around it. As she walked past Mike's boat she looked to see if there was any sign that he was on it, but there wasn't. As she continued to walk along she looked down again. She was stopped in her tracks as she caught sight of a flash of bright yellow between the boards. The moment that she saw it, she knew what she had found.

Suzie thought about leaving it there and calling the police. But what if she was wrong and she called the police for nothing. It was on the ground underneath the deck and she couldn't reach it from where she was standing, but the killer must have been able to hide it there so there must have been a way to retrieve it. She walked to the side edge of the dock and bent down. She tried to reach her arm under the wood to get the item, but she couldn't reach far enough. Suzie knew why the police had missed it, it was pretty well hidden. She lay on her stomach and extended her whole arm under. She touched something slimy and let out a silent scream, but she didn't stop trying to get the item. She needed to reach it.

With the edge of her fingertips she managed to catch a corner of the material. When she slowly pulled it up she was holding the edge of the sleeve of a bright yellow jacket. Her heart pounded as she noticed traces of blood on the hem and sleeve of the jacket. Was this it? Was this the same jacket that the killer had worn?

Suzie slowly got to her feet and with a trembling hand she reached into her pocket for her phone. She dialed Jason's number and waited for him to answer. As the phone rang several times, she noticed a shadow further along the dock. Her heart jumped. What if it was the killer and he saw her standing there with his jacket in her hand? She panicked and climbed aboard Paul's boat. Jason didn't answer. She tried calling the police station to see who was on duty, however the voice that answered was unfamiliar so she said that she had called the wrong number and hung up. She didn't often need the police in the middle of the night and hadn't gotten to know the night staff.

"Suzie, what are you doing?" She jumped at the sound of Paul's voice. When she turned to face him, his eyes were wide. "I heard someone out here, I was ready to come out and toss you off the boat. What are you doing here?"

"I couldn't sleep." She cringed. "But look what I found." She held up the jacket.

"What is that?"

"It's the yellow jacket. I think it even has blood on it."

"And you brought it on my boat?" He narrowed his eyes. "Why?"

"Sh! There's someone out there."

"Who?" He looked past her to the dock.

"I don't know. I just saw a figure. That's why I jumped on your boat."

"Okay, but it isn't a good idea to have the

jacket here. I could easily be the next suspect on the list. Let's get it to Jason."

"I tried, but he's not answering his phone." She frowned. "I think I'm just going to take it over to him."

"Here, put it in this. It'll hopefully protect what evidence might still be on it." He held open a plastic bag for her to drop the jacket in. "Do you want me to come with you to Jason?"

"No, I'll be okay."

"Are you sure we shouldn't just call the police to come pick it up?"

"I don't want whoever was on the dock to know we found the jacket. Besides, if I call the police to come get it, there's no guarantee that they won't suspect both of us. I'd rather make sure it gets into the right hands."

"Okay, I trust your judgment on that. I'll walk you to your car."

"Paul, I said I would be fine." She sighed.

"And I said I'd walk you." He stepped off the boat and reached back for her hand. She followed after. On the way to the car he looked over at her.

"Do you know how dangerous it was for you to be out here in the middle of the night?"

"Paul, this overprotective stuff has to stop. I'm a grown woman, more than capable of taking care of myself."

"But it was my boat you jumped onto wasn't it?" He opened the door for her.

"Yes, it was." She kissed his cheek. "Good night, Paul."

"Good night, Suzie. If you have any trouble let me know."

"I will."

***

The drive to Jason's house wasn't very long. However, in the span of time between the docks and his house Suzie managed to fixate on the man on the dock. Was it Mike? Someone else? It was hard to tell even the man's height or build from the distance and the brief amount of time she saw him. What if he was the killer? Did he know she had the jacket? The thought made her shiver. If the killer did know, then he might just be desperate enough to hurt someone else, or disappear entirely, leaving the case unsolved.

Suzie parked outside Jason's house and immediately noticed that the porch light shone bright. When she walked towards the house, she was surprised to hear voices from inside. Her heart beat faster as she wondered if he might be in danger. When she reached the door she recognized the second voice. It was Summer. She and Jason sounded more than a little engaged in an argument.

"Why would you even say that to me? That's the point I'm trying to make." Jason's voice strained to remain at a calm level.

"It was just a question, Jason, and I think a warranted one. I don't see why it upset you so much."

Suzie clutched the plastic bag in her hand. She didn't want to eavesdrop on their fight, but she also didn't want to interrupt it. If they knew she was outside and had overheard them they might be embarrassed.

"It's not warranted. Asking me if I want to postpone the wedding? All I want to do is marry you, Summer, and the idea that you don't know that, that bothers me. Yes, I've been distracted by the case, so have you, but that doesn't change the way that I feel about you."

Suzie's eyes closed. She knew then that she couldn't give him the jacket. She couldn't interrupt the couple. However, she also couldn't keep the jacket. She made her way down off the porch and hurried back to her car. She would have to take it to the police station. It was her only option.

As Suzie drove in that direction she thought about the fight that the two were having. Without the pressure of the case maybe they would have blissfully wandered down the aisle. But then again maybe their relationship would only be strengthened by the tension they had to work through. When she walked up to the police station she noticed that the lobby was empty. There wasn't much activity in the middle of the night in the quiet town. She opened the door and stepped inside to find an unfamiliar face at the front desk.

"Can I help you?" He settled his gaze on her inquisitively.

"I need to turn in some evidence."

"Evidence?" He stood up and eyed the bag. "Where did you get that?"

"From under the walkway at the docks. I think that it is evidence in the murder that took place there."

"Oh?" He took the bag from her and looked inside. "So, why didn't you call for an officer to pick it up?"

"I thought I'd take it to Jason myself, he's my cousin. But I was unable to get hold of him."

"It would have been better if you called an officer."

"I understand." She bit into the side of her cheek to keep her frustration from spiraling out of control. "I don't mean to cause any problems, but I need to make sure this gets into evidence as soon as possible. I think there is some blood on it."

"Great." He started typing on his keyboard.

"My name is..."

"I know your name, Suzie. Jason talks about you all the time." He smiled at her. "Don't worry, I'll take care of this for you."

"Thank you." She sighed with relief and all at once she was struck by just how exhausted she was.

By the time she arrived back at Dune House she collapsed onto the couch. She didn't bother to get a blanket or even take her shoes off. As she snored Mary crept into the kitchen with the first light of dawn. She started coffee and a small breakfast without disturbing Suzie. However, when there was a sudden knock on the door Suzie nearly fell off the couch.

"What? Where am I?" Suzie blinked as the ceiling spun above her.

"It's okay, Suzie, I'll get the door." Mary patted her shoulder as she passed her by.

"Why did I sleep in the living room?" Suzie rubbed her eyes. As the night before began to resurface in her mind she finally embraced reality.

"Suzie? You okay?" Paul smiled at Mary as he brushed past her. "I've been calling all morning."

"I'm sorry." Suzie picked up her phone to see that it was dead. "I was so tired last night I must have just passed out. Are you okay?"

"Yes, but we were going to go on a boat trip this morning, remember?"

"Oh yes." She yawned and blinked a few times. "Coffee first?"

"Sounds great."

"I'll just go have a shower quickly," Suzie said as she headed upstairs to her room.

"Come sit, Paul, I'll make you some eggs and toast."

"Thank you so much, Mary."

Suzie joined them downstairs just as Mary had finished dishing up breakfast.

"That was quick," Paul said.

"I'm quick when I want coffee." Suzie smiled.

As they shared breakfast Mary updated them on the wedding plans and Suzie filled her in on the jacket she had found.

"I ended up dropping it at the police station."

"I thought you were going to take it to Jason?" Paul finished his toast.

"I did, but he was occupied."

"How so?"

"Never mind that." She forced a smile. "I just hope we can find something on our trip today."

"You two, be careful out there. There's a murderer on the loose."

"We'll be fine," Paul said.

"Just make sure you're careful with her." Mary collected the dishes.

"I will be." Paul smiled. "Though don't tell her that, she thinks I'm overprotective."

"With her you have to be. She's always getting into trouble."

"I am sitting right here." Suzie rolled her eyes. "And you're one to talk about people getting into trouble, Mary. Should I tell him about the time that..."

"No, don't do that." Mary laughed. "Just be careful."

"Don't worry, I have no interest in going for a long swim." Suzie stood up and washed the dishes that Mary piled in the sink. "I think we'd better head out though."

"I'm ready when you are." Paul stood up.

"Mary, call me if anything goes wrong with the wedding plans, okay? We're in crunch time now."

"Trust me, you will be the first person I call."

Chapter Nine

As Suzie and Paul walked to the docks Suzie tried to call Jason. She heard his voicemail.

"He's not answering."

"What happened last night?"

"I didn't want to say anything in front of Mary, because I don't want to worry her about the wedding, but Jason and Summer were fighting when I showed up. I didn't want to interrupt."

"Oh boy." He breathed out a heavy sigh. "How bad was it?"

"That's the funny part. They were fighting about how much they cared about each other. It was kind of sweet actually."

"Hm. That's a good sign." He smiled. "Do you think they're going to make it to the end of the week?"

"Yes, I think so."

"It might be a better idea to just postpone the wedding."

"No, no." Suzie shook her head. "It will ruin the magic."

"I thought you didn't believe in the magic?" He smiled.

"I believe in their magic. If they postpone the wedding, then what's to stop them from postponing it again when something else comes up?"

"You mean if someone else ends up dead?"

"Don't say it like that." She frowned. "But yes, that's what I mean. Or some other disaster happens. They picked this date for a reason. It was the day that they went on their first date. They really want the wedding to happen then."

"Well, then we better get this case solved before then."

"Good plan," Suzie said when they reached the docks. Suzie's attention shifted right away to one of the boats.

"Let's get out onto the boat." Paul started to head towards it.

"Suzie wait!" Mary's voice made her turn back to the parking lot. As Mary approached Suzie waved to her.

"Mary, what are you doing here?"

"We have a big problem."

"What is it?" Suzie studied her friend.

"The cake. It isn't going to be ready on time. I guess there is some kind of shortage of the type of chocolate that she planned to use and now they won't have it ready for the wedding."

"So, tell them to use a different chocolate."

"She won't, she says that is the only chocolate that will work in that cake. We need to order a different cake. I've been trying to reach Jason, but he's not picking up his phone. So I went by his house, and he's not there. I went by the police station, and he's not there either. I'm starting to think that he took off."

"Took off?" Suzie raised an eyebrow. "Jason, I don't think so."

"Wedding jitters?" Paul frowned. "I doubt Jason would do that."

"Then where is he?" Mary asked.

"Maybe he went to speak with Mike's wife. Or maybe he's following up on another lead. He might have forgotten to charge his phone, just like I did. Mary, I'm going to be honest, Jason isn't going to care what kind of cake it is. Just pick one out of those that Summer originally chose, and the frosting, and it will be fine."

"Okay, I'll head right over to the bakery. But if you hear from Jason, let me know. I'm worried about him."

"Jason can handle just about anything. I'm sure he's fine. But if I hear from him you'll be the first to know."

"Thanks Suzie. I'd better get to the bakery

right away." As she hurried off Paul gave Suzie's hand a tug.

"Look who's here."

"I know, I noticed right away. He's been watching us. But it looks like Pedro has his eyes on us, too." She noticed him looking at them out of the corner of his eye.

"Yeah, fishermen don't like it when people step on their turf. I want to go talk to Mike."

"Let's get going, Paul. We probably shouldn't rile him up again."

"No, I'm going to find out once and for all if he saw that man that Pedro saw. If he did, then we might be able to figure out who it was. I'm not going to let Robbie's death go unsolved because Mike has an attitude problem."

"Just remember to keep it mellow, Paul. We don't know if he's the murderer and we can't afford to add another complication to this situation."

"I'll be good, I promise."

Suzie studied him for a moment. She wasn't the slightest bit reassured. She followed him to Mike's boat. The moment that Mike spotted them headed towards him he groaned.

"What do you want?"

"Mike, I want to know if you saw a man wearing a yellow jacket hanging around Robbie's boat. Don't hold out on me or you will pay for it."

"Oh, look at you big tough guy?" He laughed. "Showing off for the girlfriend?" He rolled his eyes. "Nice try, pal, but there's not one hair on your bushy head that intimidates me."

"Enough." Suzie pushed past Paul and climbed onto the boat.

"Again with the trespassing?" Mike glared at her. "You think because you're a woman I won't throw you right into the water?"

"Watch it!"

"It's okay, Paul." Suzie turned back to Mike. "I

know that you probably want to actually. Considering the problems that you're having with your wife, you probably have a lot of anger at the moment."

"She told you about it?" He frowned.

"No, I haven't even spoken to her. I noticed that your laundry is piled up and you're sleeping on your boat. What's going on with your wife, Mike?"

"It's none of your business."

"No, it's not. But sometimes it takes a woman to explain a woman. I might be able to help give you a little insight into what's going wrong."

He sighed and rubbed his hands together. "She wants me to give up fishing."

"What?" Paul's voice softened. "Really?"

"She says I don't spend enough time with her, I'm always gone, and she's always worried. She knew what I did for a living when we got married. Now, all of a sudden it's a problem."

"Oh Mike, it's not a problem." Suzie smiled warmly at him.

"Huh? How is it not a problem?"

"She's just showing you how much she loves and values you. You see it as her trying to take away your passion. But what she's really trying to do, is hold as tight as she can to you. She's scared of losing you. Maybe you've been a little too distant lately, not taking the time to show her how much you value her. Those things add up in her mind, and soon she thinks the only way to save the marriage is to have you at her side all the time. I'm pretty sure if you just talk to her about what might be bothering her, you two can work this out."

"I never really thought about it that way. I have been distracted lately. I have more runs than I can handle sometimes." Mike's expression relaxed. "I'll talk to her about it. Maybe I need to cut back."

"Oh, and you know what? There's a perfect

opportunity for that conversation. A special romantic dinner at Dune House and a room for the night."

"I can't afford that." He scrunched up his nose.

"You don't have to. It's on the house. A little romantic evening will soften her heart to you. It's a great time for the two of you to reconnect."

"Really. For free?"

"Yes, if you tell me about the man with the yellow jacket, it will be." Suzie set her hands to her hips and looked straight into Mike's eyes. "We're all after the same thing here. Right?"

He nodded slowly. "All right. I did see him. In fact I saw him right next to Robbie's boat. I didn't know what he was up to, but I figured it had something to do with Robbie, and I didn't want to get involved."

"When did you see him?" Suzie held his gaze.

"A few hours before Robbie turned up dead

and then an hour or two before. I remember because I thought he had been snooping around for quite a while."

"And you never mentioned this before?"

"Look, it's not like I got the man's ID or something. I don't know who he is."

"Did you notice anything about him physically?"

"He was a bit thicker than most. He also had his jacket hood covering his head the second time I saw him, which was strange because it wasn't raining and it wasn't that cold."

"Anything else about him stand out?" Suzie tried to keep a soothing tone to her voice. "Maybe a hair color, a scar, something about the way he walked?"

"Sure. He had this strange wiggle to his left toe. No. It's not like I dated the guy." Mike rolled his eyes. "I told you all I could. All right?"

"All right." Suzie nodded. "Thanks for the

information. I'll make sure you and your wife have a free night at Dune House and dinner as promised. We can arrange the date for any time after this weekend. Okay?"

"Thanks. That is if I can convince her to come. I don't think me being a murder suspect is going to make her too eager."

"Don't worry about that." Suzie patted his arm. "Just cooperate with the police and focus on what you can do to remind her of just how much you care."

"Okay. I will."

As Suzie stepped off the boat, Paul offered his hand to steady her. She took it, along with a deep breath. "It seems to me that whoever this man in the yellow jacket was, he had a very strong interest in Robbie and his boat."

"Yes, let's see if we can track him down at one of these locations." He led her to his boat and they climbed on. Once they were off to sea, Paul looked over at her. "You were amazing with Mike."

"I just tried to reach his heart." Suzie shrugged. "A man like that, you can't come at him, you have to work your way around all of the anger to get to the good stuff."

"Kind of like me?"

"No, nothing like you." She kissed his cheek. "You're all good stuff, Paul. You just think you have to be tough."

"Just like you." He smiled.

"Yes." She laughed. "Just like me."

Suzie looked out at sea and suddenly felt nervous at the thought that maybe she had just invited a murderer to stay at Dune House. However, one glimpse of Paul relaxed her. As the minutes passed she relaxed more and she began to run through possibilities in her mind. As kind as she'd been to Mike, he was still a suspect. So was the man in the yellow jacket. So far the only lead they had was that it appeared that the killer was someone that knew Robbie. She hoped that retracing his steps that day might lead them right to the killer.

"Here's the first stop." Paul pulled up to a small residential dock. When he did Suzie looked out over the sloped backyard that extended from the water. To her surprise, a flash of bright yellow caught her attention. The moment she saw it she couldn't believe it, but a second later she was certain. Even from the distance she could see that the man had no hair.

"Paul, that's him! The man from the docks that Mike and Pedro saw!"

"Where?" Paul jumped off the boat onto the dock.

"There, just past the trees. See?" She pointed to a clump of trees in the yard.

"Yes, I do." Paul began to run towards the man. Suzie climbed off the boat as fast as she could. She had no idea how Paul might react once he got his hands on the man that might be responsible for Robbie's death.

Chapter Ten

By the time Suzie caught up with the man in the yellow jacket, Paul had already tackled him to the ground. He had him pinned beneath him.

"What are you doing? Let go of me! Help!" The man beneath Paul screamed as loud as he could. Suzie's gaze fixated on the bright yellow shade of his jacket.

"Stay down and I won't have to hurt you." Paul's gruff voice was strained with the force it took to hold the man down.

"Don't hurt me, please. What do you want?" The man grew still. It struck Suzie that he didn't act or speak like someone that was guilty. He didn't act like a murderer.

"Paul, let him up."

Paul stood up and kept one hand on the man's arm as he got to his feet. The man turned to look at Suzie with wide, fear filled eyes. His stricken expression combined with his slight frame made Suzie's heart drop. Suzie continued to study him, he certainly wasn't thick set like Mike had said.

"Are you okay?"

"I don't know. Why are you two doing this to me?"

"Why did you murder Robbie?" Paul held his arm tight in his grasp.

"Murder Robbie? What are you talking about? You two have the wrong man." He straightened his shoulders. "Let me go, and I won't call the police. Just let me go, and we can forget all of this ever happened."

"I don't think we can do that." Paul narrowed his eyes. "Several witnesses place you at and around Robbie's boat just hours before he was killed."

"Wait a minute, that Robbie? He's dead?" He looked between the two. "Someone killed him?"

"Someone in a bright yellow jacket with a bald

head." Paul pulled him closer.

"Wait a minute, Paul. Let's just hear him out."

"I don't know what you think you saw, or anyone else saw, but I had nothing to do with Robbie being murdered."

"What were you doing near his boat then?" Paul eased his grip on the man's arm.

"I'm a mechanic. Not a boat mechanic specifically, but an engine is an engine. Robbie asked me to look at his boat because he'd had some problems with it. That's all I did."

"How come I've never seen you around the docks before?" Paul glared at him.

"Because I'm new to the area, I used to work in Parish."

"What's your name?" Suzie pulled out her phone.

"Gill, Gill Smith. You can look it up."

Suzie typed the name into her phone and saw that Gill Smith was indeed a mechanic. "So

Robbie hired you?"

"Yes. Well, not exactly. He paid me in shellfish."

"I see." Paul met Suzie's eyes over the top of the man's head. "What repairs needed to be done?"

"How about you try telling me who you are first?" He pulled his arm from Paul's grasp. "And maybe why you tackled me?"

"I'm Paul, and this is Suzie. Robbie was a friend of mine, and I'd like to find out what happened to him. Since the description of the man last seen around his boat included a bright yellow jacket and Robbie came to this location on the day of his murder I assumed that you might be involved in his murder."

"And tackled me." He cleared his throat. "Well, you're wrong. I had nothing to do with any murder. However, someone was certainly out to get him."

"Why do you say that?" Suzie stepped closer to him.

"Because it was a new boat and the repairs I needed to do to the engine were not from wear and tear. Someone sabotaged it, on purpose."

"How can you be sure?"

"Trust me, I've been working on engines for over twenty years. I know when something is from wear and tear, and when someone wants to keep a boat from going out on the ocean. Someone did just that to Robbie's boat. He picked me up late in the morning and asked if I could listen to the sound he was hearing. So we went on a little ride around and I did hear it. I told him I'd work on it for him."

"Did you ever tell him what you found out about the boat?" Paul stepped forward. "Maybe he confronted whoever he thought sabotaged it?"

"No, I never had the chance. He had some things to do in town so he left me there. I worked on his boat, repaired it, then took my share of the shellfish out of one of his coolers that he'd left open for me. He hadn't come back. I called him, he didn't answer. So, I caught a ride back to my place with another fisherman. I had no idea what had happened until now." He lowered his eyes. "What a shame."

"Do you have any thoughts on who might have sabotaged the boat? Did Robbie mention having any problems with anyone? Maybe he was upset when he picked you up?" Suzie asked.

"I'm sorry." He shrugged. "Robbie, was just Robbie. I didn't notice anything different."

"Maybe he took a phone call? Or he mentioned having a meeting with someone later in the day?" Suzie frowned. "I'm sorry I don't mean to push, but you might have been the last person to speak with Robbie, other than his killer."

"I wish I could help more. If I had known that Robbie was going to be killed, of course I would have paid more attention. But I didn't. To me it was just a regular day. Anyway, you can check his phone and see that I called him about the boat. I left him a message to let him know that it was fixed and to call me so I could explain what had happened."

"Thanks Gill." She looked over at Paul.

"Sorry about the rough handling." Paul offered him his hand for a handshake. "I should have asked questions first."

"Yes, that would have been good." Gill ignored Paul's hand. "I hope you find out what happened to Robbie. But I had nothing to do with it."

"Thanks for your time." Suzie started to turn away, then thought better of it. She turned back. "Gill, just one more thing."

"Yes?" He looked over his shoulder at her.

"Did you happen to lose your jacket at the dock?" The bright yellow jacket he wore was almost identical to the one she found by the docks.

She thought that maybe he had replaced it with a new one or had two of them.

"No. I only have this one." He brushed the sleeves of his jacket. "My daughter bought it for me a couple of years ago."

"Okay, thanks again." Suzie followed Paul back to the boat. As they drifted at the dock she leaned against the railing.

"Do you believe him?" Paul turned on the boat's engine.

"I'm not sure." Suzie stared at the backyard as they drifted away from it. "On one hand, maybe. He clearly didn't act guilty of anything."

"I feel awful for tackling him." Paul grimaced. "I guess I should have thought that through."

"It wasn't the best, but no harm was done. Don't let it get to you. You didn't know that he might not be the right guy."

"Might not? What makes you suspicious? He said he took the shellfish out of the cooler, that's why it was left open. He also said he got a ride on a different boat. That explains his disappearing act."

"But why did I find a yellow jacket with blood on it?" Suzie shook her head. "That's what I can't figure out. If it wasn't Gill who wore the jacket, then who did?"

"Maybe someone saw him around the dock and decided to frame him for the murder."

"You could be completely right about that. I hadn't even considered it. Someone might have framed him, and I was ready to fall right into it."

"It's a stretch, but the yellow jacket does make me wonder. Maybe someone used it as a cover to get onto the boat. Maybe Robbie only saw the yellow jacket at first and thought it was Gill."

"Maybe. Where are we headed now?"

"I'm just following what was in the GPS I have no idea what he would be going out to this location for. There's practically nothing there."

"I'm going to try Jason again. I want to make sure that he knows about Gill."

"You can try, but reception isn't always great out this way."

Suzie dialed the number and waited for Jason to pick up. As Paul had predicted the call did not go through.

"How much further, Paul? Maybe once we're on land again I can get a signal."

"Just about ten minutes." When he got closer to the location he slowed the boat.

"Oh, look at that, I guess there is some property out here. This must be where Robbie went. We should have a look." Paul squinted in an attempt to read a small no trespassing sign.

"We better be cautious we might get into trouble if we get out and walk up to the building?" Suzie said.

"We should be fine. Just stick close to me. We don't know what we might be walking into."

"I will." Suzie was always cautious from her days as an investigative journalist, but that never stopped her from investigating.

Paul stepped off the boat onto the rocky shore first. Then he reached back for Suzie's hand. She leaned on him to steady herself on the slippery rocks. In the distance there was a long, single story building. It was very plain on the outside, similar to a warehouse.

"You said you didn't know this was here?"

"No, but I haven't been out this way in a long time."

"Let's see if we can figure out what this place is." As she started to walk towards the building, something she spotted out of the corner of her eye caught her attention. It was a long, black cylinder that sunk into the water just beyond the shore. "Paul, what do you think this is?" She crouched down beside it. Paul crouched down as well.

"I'm not sure, but don't..." Suzie reached out and pulled the cylinder out of the water before

Paul could finish his sentence. Classical piano music filled the air.

"It's a speaker?" She raised an eyebrow. "Why in the world would anyone be playing music under the water?"

"Don't you touch my babies!"

Suzie looked up to see the barrel of a shotgun pointed at her. Her heart dropped.

"Suzie, get back." Paul lunged in front of her. The man who wielded the gun looked to her as if he was only a few years into his twenties. His stringy hair was pinned beneath an old, faded baseball cap.

"Please, we don't want any trouble." Suzie raised her hands in the air. The speaker splashed back into the water.

"No, you just didn't want to get caught, but you have, so now you're going to pay."

"That's enough, son, put down the gun." Paul started to stand up.

"Don't you move a muscle, old man, or I'll make sure that you never get back on your boat." Suzie put a hand on Paul's shoulder to restrain him. His protective instincts were likely trying to convince him to tackle the man. But Suzie could see from the wild look in the man's eyes that he was not bluffing.

"Nobody is going anywhere. You're in charge here. My name is Suzie, what's yours?" She kept her voice as soft as possible.

"Like a thief is going to tell me her real name. You two just sit tight until the police get here. Then you're going to pay back every dime for the pearls you've stolen from my family."

"This is all a misunderstanding. My cousin, is a police officer in Garber. Maybe you know him? Jason?"

"Jason is your cousin?" He lowered the gun some, but kept it pointed in her direction.

"Yes. I took over Dune House in Garber. Have you been in town to see it since the remodel?"

"Yes." He lowered the gun a little more. "If you own that place, why are you stealing my oysters?"

"I'm not." Suzie narrowed her eyes. "Has someone been stealing them?"

"Yes." He looked over at Paul for a long moment then finally lowered his gun the rest of the way. "I thought that's what you were doing."

"Not at all." Paul met his eyes. "We are here about the death of a friend of mine. I didn't even realize this was a pearl farm. You haven't been out here too long have you?"

"No, we haven't, just over a year. If people keep stealing from us we won't be out here much longer either. Who's your friend?"

"Robbie Stillswell."

"Robbie." He narrowed his eyes. "I've met him before. What happened to him?"

"He was killed," Paul said. "We're not sure by whom."

"I'm sorry. That doesn't explain why you're here."

"We're here because this location was listed on his GPS as a place that he traveled to. Have you spoken to him recently?" Suzie asked.

"Here? No. He'd have no reason to be here that I know of." He shook his head. "I could check with my mother."

"Is she available now?"

"Sure. Follow me." He turned and walked towards a path. Suzie hesitated for a moment. Was it safe? The man had pulled a gun on them just a few minutes before. She grabbed Paul's arm.

"Do you think we should go with him?"

"We're out here. If he tries anything, I'll put him down."

She shook her head and smiled at him. "So tough. I guess you can snatch a bullet out of midair, too?"

"I sure would try." He wrapped an arm around her shoulders. "Let's catch up, I'm not too keen on the idea of getting lost out here."

"Why do you think Robbie would have come here?" Suzie asked.

"I have no idea. Maybe he got lost."

She nodded and they walked together down the path. Not far along she noticed a large house that looked similar to Dune House only on a smaller scale. There was a sign with an arrow pointing towards the house. The sign said 'Inn'.

"An inn in the middle of nowhere. Why is that?"

"It's probably because it's a good way to maintain a profit if the pearl turnout is low. Many people would like the secluded area and beautiful beaches."

"Do you think that Robbie might have stayed here? That might be why this location was on his GPS."

"It might be. Or maybe he came here to visit someone who stayed here or works here."

"It's possible, or maybe he even got lost."

"Wait here, I'll get my mother." He ascended the wide porch. Suzie lingered beside Paul and watched as the man disappeared inside the house.

"I've never even heard of a pearl farm before," Suzie said.

"It's not too common around here. In fact this is the only one I know of in this area. They haven't been around very long and must be trying to get a foothold."

"It's funny though, I've never really thought about how pearls are harvested. Is that why there was a speaker in the water?"

"Uh, that seems a little odd to me, but I'm sure they have a reason." Paul smiled.

The front door opened and a small-statured woman stepped out. She had long, gray hair that hung loose around her shoulders and well past her waist.

"What is it?" She put her hands on her hips. "This is private property you know."

"We're only here to ask a few questions." Suzie stepped forward. She assumed that perhaps the woman would be more comfortable speaking with her, than with Paul.

"Do I look like a librarian to you? If you want information, that's who you should talk to."

"We don't mean to bother you, but this is in regards to a murder investigation. Do you think you could spare a few minutes to answer some questions?"

"Murder investigation? Who's dead?" She narrowed her eyes.

"A friend of mine." Paul removed his hat and stepped forward. "Robbie, a fisherman."

"Robbie? Oh, he was just a young man. I've met him a few times. But why do you want to ask me questions about him?"

"This location was listed on his GPS. Do you have any idea why that might be?"

"Well, I can't really say. I haven't spoken to him. But we do have guests that stay here. I don't keep track of their visitors. Just about the only way to get out here is by boat. The dirt track takes ages. Maybe he came by to meet with someone."

"You don't keep records of the boats that come in and out?"

"No. We barely have anyone come out here anyway."

"Your son greeted us with a gun. Is that how you always greet guests?"

"We weren't expecting any new guests. However, over the past couple of weeks we've had someone stealing some of our pearls. I'm sure Junior just assumed that might be you, since you two decided to show up without calling ahead and we weren't expecting anyone. A courtesy call could have prevented all of those problems."

"Fair enough." Suzie nodded. "What about your guest registry? Could we see a copy of that?"

"Sure. I'll get it for you. Just wait here." She went back into the house.

"See? Not too bad." Paul smiled at Suzie.

"You do know she's not coming back, right?" She raised an eyebrow.

"She's coming back." Paul looked towards the door. "Any second now."

Suzie glanced at her watch. Then she looked back at him. After a few minutes passed she glanced at her watch again.

"All right, all right." Paul sighed. "You were right. She's not coming back."

"Should we knock?"

"If she's not going to cooperate there's no point. I'm sure that Jason will have better luck getting the information from her. Let's keep going to the list of locations."

As she walked back towards the boat Suzie

thought about the thefts at the pearl farm. By the time she reached the boat she knew that she was going to have to broach the subject with Paul.

"Do you think that Robbie might have been the one stealing the pearls?"

Paul gritted his teeth as he helped her on board. "I'd rather not think that."

"I don't know. Remember that he was coming and going at odd hours."

"Says Mike, who is our prime suspect."

"Not just Mike."

"Suzie, until we get solid information that he was involved, I don't even want to consider it."

"All right." Suzie nodded and settled into silence as he pulled up the next location on the GPS.

"There's not much point to going out to Simon's place. If Robbie went out to see him it was just to visit. Simon's been a friend of ours for years."

"Still, it might be good to find out what he spoke to Simon about, or whether Robbie acted strangely. We did see Simon's boat pulling away right before we found Robbie."

"That's true. I wouldn't mind checking in with Simon anyway. If we're lucky he might offer us lunch. He has a way with seafood, it's always been the best I've ever tasted."

"Mm, sounds delicious." Suzie settled into a seat and stared out at the water.

Chapter Eleven

As Suzie and Paul sailed towards Simon's place Suzie was lost in thought as she looked out at the large expanse of water. In her mind she tried to form a timeline of what might have happened from the time that Robbie launched in the morning until the time he docked and met his murderer. It was hard to place exactly where he was at what time as the GPS only recorded the time when the boat stopped at the specific coordinates, and not how long the boat was in each particular location.

The fact that Robbie's death came not long after there were a few thefts at the pearl farm was something that Suzie could not shake. Could it really just be a coincidence? She knew that Paul wanted to believe his friend was an honest person, but some of the information she'd gathered so far about him, indicated that he might lead a different lifestyle than Paul was aware of.

"Not far now." Paul slowed the boat. Suzie stood up and watched as they approached a short dock. The dock was littered with lounge chairs, coolers, and fishing poles. It looked very well used. Paul eased the boat to a stop. "Let me just give him a call and let him know we're here."

As Paul made the call Suzie focused on every detail of the dock. If it was one of the last places that Robbie had been, there might be a clue as to what had happened to him.

"Hey buddy, it's Paul. I'm at your dock. Are you free?" Paul looked over at Suzie and nodded. "Sure we'll be right up. Yes, I brought her." He chuckled. Suzie raised an eyebrow as he hung up the phone. "He's looking forward to meeting you." He grinned. "I think he thought I'd made you up."

"Really?" Suzie laughed. "That's silly."

Paul smiled and gave her a light hug, then climbed off the boat. He turned back to help her off as well. They walked up a small hill to a single story house. It didn't look like it was in the best repair. The yard was scattered with half-finished projects and piles of wood that waited to be chopped. Music drifted through the open windows of the house. Suzie recognized the melody. It seemed to her that Simon had an affection for classical music. Paul led her up to the back door of the house. He knocked once, then opened the door.

"Come on in the kitchen, Paul!" Simon's voice bellowed from around the corner. Paul took her hand and turned down the hall to the kitchen. A wonderful scent greeted her just before a man with only an apron for a shirt walked towards her with his arms wide open. "You must be Suzie!" He wrapped his arms around her before she had the chance to stop him. Not only did he hug her, he lifted her right up off the ground. When he released her she plopped back down on the ground with a laugh.

"Nice to meet you too, Simon."

"Sorry, I should have warned you, he's a little

physical." Paul put his hands up before Simon could hug him, but Simon still wrestled his arms around him. "How are you, pal? I haven't seen you in a while."

"I know, I've been a little, occupied."

"I can see that." Simon chuckled. "Lucky man. You two hungry? I've got lunch on the stove ready to go."

"That would be great." Paul nodded.

"Sure, just settle in, I'll get you some plates." As Suzie and Paul sat down at the table Simon tossed a pack of paper plates towards them. Paul pulled some out.

"Did you hear about Robbie?"

Simon froze, then turned to face Paul. "I figured that might be why you were here. I heard."

"I should have called you." Paul frowned.

"It's all right. It's hard to talk about."

"You saw him yesterday?" Suzie met his eyes. "How did he seem to you?"

"I didn't see him yesterday." He sat down across from them with a plate filled with an assortment of seafood.

"Oh? The GPS on his boat said he traveled here," Suzie said.

"Well, I must have missed him. What a shame. I was out fishing yesterday. I wonder why he stopped by?"

"It's hard to say." Paul shook his head. "He was probably just coming by to say hello."

"Maybe." Simon narrowed his eyes. "I wish I knew though. It's hard to think of someone's last hours, and knowing that they wanted to see you, but didn't get the chance."

"It is." Paul took a bite of his food.

"We saw you leaving the Garber docks yesterday. Didn't you see him then?" Suzie asked.

"No." He shook his head. "I never docked. I just passed nearby on my way back home from fishing."

148

"Do you know anything about that pearl farm in the area?" Suzie nibbled some of her food and then took a larger bite. Paul was right, it was the best she'd ever tasted.

"Uh, I heard about it." He nodded. "The word around town is that they're struggling. They are real reclusive folk. Not the type to make friends with. So, I've kept my distance."

"I didn't even know they were out there." Paul shook his head. "Just discovered them today. Can you think of any business that Robbie might have had out there?"

"At the pearl farm?" He spoke between bites of food. "No, not really."

"Do you remember that girl that he was sweet on?" Paul laughed. "Maybe she was from the farm."

"Oh, that's right?" Simon nodded. "Maybe she was."

"Really?" Suzie raised an eyebrow. "She

seems a bit old for him."

"No, this girl is young, she's probably about twenty. He had a thing for her," Simon said. "I don't think she was from the pearl farm but maybe she was. I don't know if he ever approached her."

"Do you remember her name?" Suzie asked.

"He mentioned it, but I don't." Simon shook his head.

"I think it was April? Or May? Some calendar name." Paul shrugged. "I think we can rule out December." He laughed. Suzie looked over at him with an amused smile. He seemed so relaxed around Simon.

"If you happen to remember can you let Paul know?" Suzie looked at Simon. "That crowd over there is not very welcoming, and since we were greeted by a gun, there's a good chance they had something to do with Robbie's death."

"It's a shame." Simon hung his head. "He was

just starting out really. Could have done well for himself. I guess he stuck his nose into something he shouldn't have."

"Why do you say that?" Suzie locked eyes with him.

"Ain't that always how someone ends up dead?" He stared back at her with a gaze so cold that her heart dropped. She glanced over at Paul to see if he had noticed, but Paul was too busy taking the last few bites of his food to notice. She shivered and lowered her eyes. Maybe it was just her imagination, but it seemed to her that Simon meant his words as a threat.

When they had finished up their meal Simon led them out into the back. He talked to Paul about all of the projects he planned to finish. Suzie tuned out as she sorted through her own thoughts. Was she overreacting to the way that Simon had spoken to her?

"I guess we'd better head out." Paul placed a hand on the small of Suzie's back. "Don't want to be out in the dark."

"I heard that there's a fierce storm rolling in tomorrow. Keep an eye out for it," Simon said.

"I will." Paul nodded. "Thanks for the warning."

"Wait. We should get a picture." Suzie pulled out her phone and smiled as the two men huddled around her. As she snapped the selfie she reminded herself that Simon was a friend of Paul's, and that meant she needed to give him the benefit of the doubt. She tucked her phone back into her pocket. "It was really nice meeting you, Simon."

"You too." He smiled and winked at her. "You might have to throw an anchor around this one to keep him on land, but it'll be worth it."

"Ah, that's where you're wrong, Simon. Not even an anchor would keep me out of the ocean. Luckily, Suzie understands. Don't you, Suzie?" He glanced over at her.

"Yes, I do. I would never keep him away." She patted his chest and smiled as she looked into his eyes.

"Good woman." Simon nodded and stared at them both for a moment then gestured to the dock. "I'd walk you down, but I've got to clean up. Have a good trip back."

"Thanks, Bud." Paul gave him a light shove on the shoulder then slipped his arm through Suzie's. As they walked back towards the boat Suzie considered mentioning her concerns, but it had been such a nice visit, she didn't want to add tension. She kept quiet for the ride back to the docks. When Paul cut off the engine he looked over at her.

"Okay, what is it?"

"What?" She smiled.

"You are never this quiet."

"Don't be silly, I'm quiet all of the time."

"No, you certainly aren't. Especially when

you're investigating something."

"Okay, okay. I am a bit more quiet than usual."

"So? What is it?" He met her eyes.

"It's just Simon."

"Simon? What about him?"

"Did you notice anything off about him?"

"No, not really. Did you?"

"I'm not sure. Something about the way he talked to me, warning me to stay out of other people's business, really left me flustered."

"Oh, Simon can be that way." Paul frowned. "I'm sorry I didn't notice that. But he can be a bit harsh."

"Do you think he knows something about what happened to Robbie?"

"If he did, he would tell me." Paul narrowed his eyes. "He would want Robbie's murderer brought to justice."

"Are you sure? I mean, it looks like Robbie was up to some things that you didn't know about. Maybe Simon is hiding things, too."

"Suzie, I respect your instincts, I truly do, but just because Simon is a little rough around the edges, that doesn't mean that he had anything to do with Robbie's death."

"I know that, you're right. I just think it was a little odd the way he spoke about some things."

"Today is the first time that you met him, so I can understand that. His type of charm is something that has to grow on you."

"I understand, I guess I'm a little paranoid. Hopefully we can find something out about the people at the pearl farm. If so we might be able to get to the bottom of things."

"I want to check in with some of Robbie's friends. Some of his family is also supposed to be coming into town."

"Do you want me to come with you?" Suzie

met his eyes.

"No, thanks. I just want to make sure they have everything they need."

"I'll go and update Jason."

"Good idea." He glanced over at her. "Are you okay?"

"Of course I am. Why?"

"The gun thing." He frowned.

"No, I'm fine. You were there with me, right?"

He smiled. "That I was."

"Then I'm fine." She kissed his cheek.

"Do you want a lift?"

"No thank you, I could use the walk." Suzie smiled. "Let me know if the family needs anything."

"I will." As Suzie walked away she tried to convince herself that he was right. Simon had nothing to do with what had happened to Robbie and had no information to offer. Her instincts were off. But she couldn't shake the feeling that she was right.

Chapter Twelve

By the time Suzie reached the police station she'd already decided to tell Jason about Simon. When she walked up to Jason's desk he had his phone trapped between his ear and his shoulder. She noticed the way his brow furrowed, and the ripple of his jaw. His shoulders were hunched over and his skin was pale.

"Do whatever it takes, and just get it done." He frowned as he hung up the phone and ran his hands across his face.

"Are you okay?"

"Yes I'm fine, just busy."

"Let me know if you need help with anything."

"All right, what can I do for you?"

"Paul and I took a ride around today to the places that Robbie last went to just to see if there was anything interesting out there."

"Why doesn't that surprise me? I had second

thoughts about giving Paul a copy of the coordinates. I hope you didn't antagonize anyone or jeopardize the investigation?"

"No of course not, but there were a couple of things of concern. One, at one of the places Robbie went to we found a man in a yellow jacket that has a bald head. He matches the description of someone that was seen hanging around Robbie's boat on the day he was murdered. Apparently, he was repairing Robbie's boat."

"Yes, I know, I spoke with him just before."

"And you have the jacket I brought in last night?"

"Yes. I'm going with the idea that someone else in a yellow jacket was the one who actually killed Robbie. But I'm not sure of that yet. It's possible that Gill bought another jacket to replace the one he damaged. Or the murderer deliberately tried to frame Gill by planting a yellow jacket."

"That would make sense. But maybe there would be a paper trail that we could follow to see if Gill purchased it recently?"

"Maybe, but if he bought it with cash it won't be likely. And it would be quite a difficult trail to follow. I plan to ask him for a DNA sample and we can compare that to what we find on the jacket."

"What about the blood? Is it Robbie's?"

"That hasn't been confirmed yet, but at the moment I'm assuming it is."

"Have you spoken to the people at the pearl farm?"

"Oh yes, that's another can of worms. I made some inquires with the police department where the family that owns the pearl farm used to live. Apparently Cecily Wren, the owner of the farm, has a long history of run-ins with the law. She's even been arrested for breaking and entering before. Her son, Junior, is no better. He's had some assault charges brought against him."

"Not surprising, since he pulled a gun on us."

"What?" His eyes widened.

"Don't worry about it, we handled it. Apparently they've had some thefts at their farm and he assumed we might be involved."

"Hm. They haven't reported any here. Someone is stealing from criminals. Good to know."

"Easy Jason, they could be turning their lives around. You never know."

"Sure, you're right." He sighed. "Did you discover anything else?"

"Well, we went to the last place on the GPS and it turned out to be a friend of both Paul's and Robbie's. His name is Simon."

"Right, I know him and I've spoken to him and there doesn't seem to be any reason to suspect him. Paul also told me that he wouldn't be an issue."

"I know that Paul feels that way, but I have to wonder."

"Why do you have to wonder?" Jason leaned forward some and looked into her eyes. "Your instincts are usually on target, Suzie, let me know what you're thinking."

"It's just that Simon claimed not to have seen Robbie. Then he gave me this look, and a warning about sticking my nose in other people's business."

"He threatened you?"

"No, I couldn't exactly say that. But I did feel like it was a threat. Just the way he said it, and the way he looked at me, made me think that he was warning me not to get into his business."

"It's not unusual for fishermen to behave like that. They like their privacy."

"You're right. Still, I think it might be best to confirm his whereabouts. Paul also mentioned something about Robbie having a crush on a girl and thought that maybe she was from the pearl farm. Paul and Simon couldn't remember her name, but said she was quite young and her name was a month. You know like May or...."

"That might be Cecily's niece, April. She's on the list of employees. I guess that might be why Robbie went out to the farm."

"Maybe." Suzie nodded. "I know it's not much to go on, but it's a start."

"Suzie, I know telling you to stay out of this is useless, but please be careful."

"I will be, don't worry," Suzie said. "Don't forget, Jason, you're getting married. Make sure you write your vows."

"I'm working on it, I'm working on it." He yawned.

"Good." Suzie stood up from her chair, then paused. "I know it's not my place, but I overheard you arguing with Summer last night."

"You did?" His cheeks grew red. "I figured that was why you didn't give me the jacket."

"I just want you to know, it's normal to fight. Fighting means you care enough to struggle. If you're not fighting, that's when you should worry."

"You know this from your vast experience?"

"Okay, you've got me there. But I know how much you two love each other, and I don't want you to get discouraged."

"Thanks Suzie." He smiled, but the expression faded quickly. "I'll check into Simon and see if I come up with anything. In the meantime I'm running down a few leads from the docks. I'll be honest though, something is missing here. Normally there would be a thread, a piece of evidence that points me in the right direction. I just don't feel like I have that yet."

"Hopefully something will turn up soon."

"Hopefully."

"I'll let you know if I hear anything new."

"Thanks Suzie." He picked up his phone again and began to dial a number. Suzie left the station and walked towards Main Street. The events of the day tumbled through her mind. Due to her investigative mind if she encountered anything that she didn't have a base knowledge of, it hung in her mind until she learned more about it. She knew nothing about pearls, or pearl farms, or what anyone would do with stolen pearls. If she had questions, she thought the best place to go would be the jewelry shop. But before she headed there she decided to get a bottle of water. Her throat was dry from being out in the sea air. She stepped into the convenience store and grabbed a bottle out of one of the coolers. She pulled out her phone and dialed Mary's number.

"Hi Mary."

"Suzie? How is everything?"

"Okay. I'm just going to the jewelry shop in town, I have a couple of questions to ask Nina."

"Oh good, I'll meet you there. I need to speak to her about the rings."

"The wedding rings?" Suzie paused a few feet from the register. "Is there a problem?"

"No problem. Jason wants to add an inscription to the rings, but he's very busy on the case, so he asked if I could stop in."

"Okay, see you soon." Suzie hung up the phone and set the bottle down on the counter. She smiled at the woman behind the counter, Suzie knew her from the convenience store but she didn't know her name.

"Looks like you've been out on the boat all day."

"Oh?" Suzie reached up to touch her hair, but the woman shook her head.

"You've got some sunburn. Might want to get some aloe on that."

Suzie touched her cheek and felt the heat against her fingertips. There was no question that she had sunburn. She grimaced at the thought. "Thanks for the warning." She was about to walk away when she hesitated. "Did you hear about the fisherman that was killed on his boat?"

"Yes." She lowered her eyes and shook her head. "Just awful."

"Yes, it is."

"I had just seen him that day. He came in here."

"Really. Did you notice anything strange?"

"It was early in the morning so I was rushing around getting the coffee pots ready. He and his friend waited for me to have a pot ready." She frowned. "It's so odd that a person can be right in front of you one day and then gone."

"Yes it is. You mentioned he was with a friend. Did you know who the friend was? A woman?"

"No, a man. Uh, what's his name?" She narrowed her eyes. "He's hard to forget but his name, I just can't think of it right now."

"How come he was hard to forget?"

"Kind of loud. A burly guy you know. Oh that's it, Simon." She nodded. "That's his name."

"Simon?"

"Yes."

"Are you sure it was the day Robbie died?"

"Yes, I'm sure. I gave them the first cups of coffee out of the pot. They seemed tense and I wanted to get them out of the store."

"Tense how?"

"They kept talking real low, but the tone was hard, you know, angry." She frowned. "I don't know. I didn't hear anything specific."

"Okay, thanks for the info."

"Sure, I hope they figure out who did it."

Suzie picked up her water and headed out the door. As she did she dialed Jason's number. The phone rang several times, but he didn't answer. She hung up and tried Paul's number. He didn't pick up, either. She shoved her phone back into her pocket and sighed. If Simon was in the store with Robbie, why did he claim that he hadn't seen Robbie? It was clear to her that Simon had lied to her, and after the way he had looked at her, she was sure that he was trying to hide something. As her mind still swirled she made her way towards the jewelry store.

Chapter Thirteen

A friend of Summer's worked at the jewelry store. Maybe she would be willing to give Suzie a quick tutorial about pearls. Suzie pulled open the door to the jewelry store and stepped inside. The carpet was plush and the lights were bright. A woman waved to her as she walked towards one of the glass display cases.

"Hi Suzie."

"Hi Nina. I wonder if I could have a minute of your time."

"Sure, just give me a couple of minutes I have some paperwork to fill out, then I'll be all yours."

"Thanks." Suzie nodded at her. She had met Nina a few times, but didn't know her very well. Suzie looked into the display cases while she waited. A large display of pearl jewelry held her attention. She didn't think it was too unusual, but the fact that she had just been to a pearl farm for the first time made the jewelry stand out to her. She'd never been much of a fan of pearls, but she found herself admiring them just a little more. The door to the jewelry shop opened and Suzie turned to see Mary step inside.

"Hi Mary." Suzie smiled and gestured for Mary to join her. "Have you seen this collection?"

"No, I haven't." Mary peered through the glass. "It's beautiful. The one gift Kent gave me that I truly treasured was a pearl pendant. I don't know why, but they always made me feel so refined."

"I've never seen you wear pearls." Suzie raised an eyebrow.

"I never had much of a reason to be refined. I left it with him when I moved away. It might have been beautiful, but it was still a reminder I didn't need."

"I understand." Suzie looked back at the display. "I was at a pearl farm today and they mentioned some recent thefts. I thought perhaps

Nina could tell me a little bit about the pearls."

"I sure can." Nina paused behind the display. "These came from the Atlantic."

"You know where they come from?" Suzie looked up at her.

"Absolutely. We're always very careful who we purchase the pearls from. Is that what you wanted to talk to me about?"

"Yes. Did you know there's a farm in the area, close to Parish?"

"Oh yes, I just recently heard about them."

"You didn't purchase any pearls from them?"

"No. We only deal with large, reputable farms. It's too hard to tell whether small farms are using legal, ethical and safe practices when harvesting their pearls and we don't want to support anything that our customers wouldn't be happy with."

"That's a good thing. So, no one tried to sell your shop any pearls?"

"It's not uncommon for some of the local fishermen to try to sell pearls that they've happened to come across if the pawn shop won't take them. I mean Frank and Pedro have been in here a few times as well as some others that I don't know the names of. There seems to be quite a few pearls around lately. However, there was a man in here the other day that tried to sell me a larger amount than usual. I've seen him before, but I don't know his name and I turned him away. When I asked him about them he couldn't give me a clear explanation of where they came from."

"Interesting. I wonder if they might have been stolen from the pearl farm. They've had several thefts lately."

"Hm. Maybe. I had no reason to believe they were stolen otherwise I would have let Jason know."

"You said it was a man?" Suzie pulled her phone out of her pocket. "Was it this man?" She showed her a picture of Gill Smith from his website.

"No. That's not him."

"How about this man?" She scrolled to a picture of Mike that she had secretly taken.

"No, sorry, not him either."

As Suzie began scrolling through pictures to get to a photograph she'd managed to get from the internet of Robbie, Nina gasped. "That's him right there!" She pointed at a picture from earlier that day of Paul with his arm around her and Simon just beside him.

"Paul?" Mary blurted out. "That can't be right."

"No, not Paul. Him." She pointed directly at Simon. "He was the one that tried to sell me the pearls."

"Are you certain?"

"Yes. I could pull the footage from the security cameras, but I'm afraid you won't be able to see much. He only showed me the pearls briefly before I asked him to leave. I don't think the cameras caught it. But they will show him."

"Thank you so much. I'll see if Jason wants to send an officer over to collect the footage."

"Sure, any time."

"Speaking of Jason." Mary stepped forward. "He would like this inscription added to the wedding rings." She handed Nina a slip of paper. "Is it too late to do that?"

"Not for Summer and Jason." Nina smiled. "I'll make sure that it gets done right away."

"Thanks." Mary sighed with relief. "At least one thing is going right."

"What is going wrong?" Suzie stepped out the door behind Mary.

"A few of the flights were delayed for some of Summer's family members and a couple of friends and so I've had to rearrange the pick-ups. Not to mention that the fresh linens aren't on the beds yet and I haven't made it to the grocery store to pick up the extra supplies..."

"Oh Mary, I got so caught up in all of this I've been leaving everything on your shoulders. I'm sorry for that. I'll take care of the linens as soon as we get home and once that is done I'll go to the store. You just focus on the guests coming in and if you need any help with making the arrangements let me know."

"Suzie, you don't have anything to apologize for, what you're doing is very important. If the murder is solved then at least Summer and Jason can relax at the wedding. With the tension at the moment I'm worried that there won't even be a wedding."

"Don't talk like that." Suzie wrapped an arm around her shoulders. "There is going to be a wedding, even if I have to tie the two of them down to make it happen."

"Hm, I'm pretty sure that's illegal."

"Someone has to arrest me, and since Jason will be tied up, who's left?"

Mary laughed and shook her head. "You always know how to lighten my mood, Suzie. But I hope you're right, Jason and Summer deserve a wedding without any problems."

"Has a wedding like that ever happened?"

"If not, then I'm determined to make this one the first."

"If you're determined, Mary, then I have no doubt that it will happen."

Chapter Fourteen

Suzie shook out the sheet and spread it across the bed. The scent of the laundry soap and the subtle breeze created by the movement brought a smile to her lips. As she tucked in the corners her cell phone began to ring. She rushed over to it and picked it up.

"Paul, I've been trying to reach you."

"I know you have, I'm sorry, Suzie. I got caught up with Robbie's sister and it just didn't seem right to excuse myself for a phone call. Is everything okay?"

"I'm not sure. I know you think that Simon had nothing to do with this, but he lied to us."

"What do you mean?"

"He said he hadn't seen Robbie, but the clerk at the convenience store told me that he was in there with Robbie the day he died."

"Maybe she was mistaken?"

"No, she was pretty broken up about the fact that she was one of the last people to see him alive. She was certain it was that morning and that it was Simon."

"It's possible that Simon just overlooked it. Maybe it was just a chance meeting."

"Maybe. But then Nina at the jewelry store said that he tried to sell her some pearls. Quite a large amount, apparently."

"What? Why would Simon have pearls? He doesn't deal in pearls."

"I have no..." Suzie said then stopped and her eyes widened. "Wait a minute, I think I know."

"You do?"

"Yep. The girl that Robbie liked, she does work at the pearl farm. Her name is April, according to Jason. Maybe she gave Robbie and Simon some pearls. Maybe she's behind this and she's stealing the pearls for them."

"You could be onto something. I find it hard

to believe that Simon or Robbie would be involved in this, but maybe April was involved somehow."

"The family does have an extensive criminal history."

"I think we should look into it more," Paul said.

"Good idea. I have to do some shopping and then if you want we could try going out to the pearl farm again."

"Do you really think that's a good idea? After what happened out there earlier? It's not as if they're going to be willing to talk to us."

"That's true. I wonder if we can find another way to get to April. Let me do some checking while I'm in town. Does Robbie's family have any idea who might be behind this?"

"No, not that they told me. How is everything going with the wedding plans?"

"It's coming together."

"Good, let me know when you want to meet

up."

"I will." Suzie hung up the phone and finished making the beds. As she worked one by one through the rooms to make sure that each one was in order she wondered if the footage from the jewelry store would be good enough to identify Simon. If it wasn't then it might come down to eye witness identification. Would Paul believe it? She thought he was making excuses for a friend who might not have been much of a friend after all. She did one last check in the kitchen to be sure that everything on the grocery list was all that they needed. As she headed for the door Mary rushed towards her.

"Suzie, I'm so glad that I caught you. I need a few more things from the store. Some of the guests have made some requests and after being delayed and all the trouble at the airport I want to accommodate them as much as possible."

"I agree, just let me know what you need."

"Here, I made another little list." She handed

it to her and took a deep breath. "I think we're just about ready."

"Wonderful. I'll have the groceries back here in no time." Suzie left Dune House with a sense of urgency. With the guests arriving and the wedding day drawing closer, it seemed as if everything was closing in.

As she pulled into the parking lot of the grocery store she was so distracted that she almost drove into a stray cart. She hit the brakes hard and stared as it rolled by pushed by the wind. It wasn't the sight of the cart that startled her as much as it was her lack of attention. Shaken, she parked the car and walked into the store. She focused on the list of items and made sure she didn't forget anything. When she joined the line to the only open register her cell phone rang. She saw that it was Jason, and since the line was so long she decided to answer it.

"Jason, did you find out anything new?"

"Not much on Simon, he's a pretty private

person. Is Paul with you by any chance?"

"No."

"Oh, I tried to get hold of him, but I couldn't. Summer did let me know that Robbie was most likely not killed with a weapon, it was more likely a tool."

"Like a screwdriver?"

"Something like that only short, flat, pointy at the tip but then it gets wider. It's hard to describe exactly. She hasn't been able to find a weapon that matches it, so her best guess is that it's a tool of some kind. That's why I was hoping Paul was with you to ask him if he knows of any tools used on a boat that matches that description."

"Hm. Interesting. I was speaking to him just before, so maybe that's why you couldn't get through." She moved forward a few steps in line. She filled him in on what she had found out at the jewelry store explaining that she had been there to meet Mary and just used the opportunity to ask about the pearls so he wouldn't think she was meddling too much. "Paul and I think that April might be involved in all of this."

"Really? She's the only one from the farm with a clean record. But I was going to get all of them in from the farm for further questioning, anyway. She's the first one on the list and she should be here in around an hour."

"Oh, okay. If she hasn't been in trouble with the law before, she might be more talkative."

"Good point. Someone is going out shortly to pick her up."

"Let me know how you go."

"I will."

Suzie hung up and pushed her cart forward in line again. She glanced at the other registers that were closed. Unless there was a big event the grocery store rarely had more than one register open. Still, she could hope. As she waited bits of conversation drifted to her ears.

"Robbie knew better. He shouldn't have

gotten mixed up in all of that."

"You don't know that for sure. Just because there are rumors doesn't make them true."

"Rumors maybe, but he was flaunting the cash. You saw his new boat, and the way he flashed money around town. It's not like he was trying to hide it."

Suzie didn't realize that she had leaned too heavily against the cart until she felt it bounce against the woman's ankle in front of her.

"Ouch!"

"I'm so sorry!" Suzie drew the cart back.

"Oh, Suzie right?" The woman smiled at her. "I bet you're getting all set for the wedding, huh?"

"Busy, busy." Suzie nodded. "It's an exciting time."

"Yes, it is. Make sure you wish Jason and Summer well from Judy."

"Are you a friend of theirs?"

"Not really, but their romance is the talk of the town."

"Among other things?" Suzie raised an eyebrow. "I'm sorry I just couldn't help but overhear what you said about Robbie."

"How embarrassing. I don't usually gossip. But it's such a sad story."

"Did you know Robbie?"

"Sure, we went to high school together. We'd say hello to each other when we saw each other in town, but nothing more than that."

"I'm sorry for your loss."

"Thank you. I just wish he'd been more careful."

"Why do you say that?"

"Well, clearly he was involved in something criminal. He started making big purchases, had a lot of money in his pocket. He didn't come right out and say it, but he might as well have."

"Maybe he just had a good run?"

"Not that good. Like I said, I grew up around here, and no fisherman no matter how good the run, has that kind of cash. You know a lot of the boats run drugs, things like that."

"A lot of them?" Suzie raised an eyebrow. "Are you sure about that?"

"Okay, that might be a bit of an exaggeration. But if you ask most of the guys that work on the boats they have stories about the illegal activity that could make them a mint."

"Stories." Suzie frowned. "Do you think they're anything more than that?"

"It's hard to say. But I can tell you the only person I've seen with that kind of money over the past few years is Robbie. It doesn't come from the ocean. Good luck with the wedding." She rolled her cart away from the register.

Suzie paid for her items and then pushed the cart out to the car. The more she heard about Robbie's recent behavior the more she suspected the same thing that some other people did. If

Robbie had some kind of windfall his family would know about it. She called Paul as she loaded the groceries into the car.

"Paul, did any of Robbie's family members mention him having some kind of windfall lately?"

"Windfall? No. They were worried about the debt they might have to deal with from the boat and dock fees."

"Paul, it sounds like Robbie was making money somewhere, and more than likely not legally."

"What are you thinking?"

"Maybe the pearl farm was on his GPS tracker because he was stealing from them."

"I hate to think that."

"Me too, but I think we have good reason to suspect him."

"It's hard for me to believe that my friend could have been involved in these things without me knowing it."

"Maybe you missed it. If people want to hide something they usually can."

"Maybe I did miss it." He sighed. "Maybe if I was around more."

"No, Paul, you can't think like that. If Robbie got himself wrapped up in something it was because of his choice, there's nothing that you could have done."

"I can do something now though. Get to the bottom of this."

"Jason is going to interview the girl from the pearl farm that Robbie might have been seeing. I might accidently bump into her while she's at the police station."

"Accidently." He laughed. "Okay, I'll wait to hear from you."

Suzie hung up the phone and started to open her car door. Before she could grasp the handle a heavy force drove her forward to the alley beside the grocery store. She panicked as the large figure behind her continued to propel her.

"Suzie, I need to talk to you." Mike's gruff voice filled her senses.

"Get off of me, Mike!" She shoved back at him. "What are you thinking?"

"The cops are all over me, asking questions, inspecting my boat. I didn't do this!"

She stared hard at Mike. "If you really want me to believe that you had nothing to do with this then you should stop doing things like this. This tough guy act isn't convincing me of anything but your bad judgment."

"It's not an act!" Mike growled.

"All you're doing is driving yourself even deeper into suspicion. Is that what you want? To get locked up?"

"No, it's not."

"Well, that's where you will be, Mike, you shoved me down here in this alley like some brute and if I wanted to I could have you in handcuffs by now. So why do you think I should believe you?"

Mike growled and ran his hands across his face. "I just want one person to believe me. I had nothing to do with this. My whole livelihood is dependent on that boat. I've never done anything wrong. If the police take it, what will I have?"

Suzie sighed and shook her head. "Stop Mike, just stop. The police are investigating the case. It's going to get sorted out."

"Right, with me as the fall guy."

"Not unless you paint a target on your back." She frowned. "I believe you. Okay? I don't think you had anything to do with this." Suzie wanted to placate the man and although her gut told her that he wasn't involved she still suspected him and she didn't want him to know that.

"Thank you. That's all I want."

"Great. Can I go now?" She peered past him at

the car.

"Yes. You'll tell Jason?"

"That you practically kidnapped and assaulted me?" She raised an eyebrow.

"No! That's not what I meant."

"I know that, Mike. But you need to lay low. Don't do anything stupid. This will all be settled soon."

"Thank you, Suzie."

She nodded and stepped around him. Despite the fact that the confrontation was over, her heart still raced so fast that it was hard to breathe. She hurried back to her car. For a moment she considered a phone call to Jason to tell him what had happened. But she didn't want to bother him.

Suzie took a deep breath and then focused on the drive back to Dune House. She dropped off the groceries, shouted a greeting and goodbye to Mary then headed back to the car. She drove straight to the station. She hoped that maybe she would be able to catch April on her way out and ask her a few questions. Maybe she would be able to get more information out of her than the police could.

When she stepped inside there was a small crowd at the front desk. She edged her way around it and was greeted by a patrolman at the entrance of the hall that led to the interrogation rooms.

"Hello there, Suzie."

"Hi." She smiled. "Just dropping by to visit Jason."

"Uh huh, and I'm just here to make sure you don't interrupt any conversations. At Jason's request."

"Really? He sent muscle?"

"Looks like his instincts were right."

"I was just checking in." She shrugged.

"Just do me a favor and stay out here in reception, hm?" He met her eyes.

"Yes, of course." She retreated a few steps towards the seating area. When he walked away a door opened and she noticed a beautiful, young woman who stepped out of it. She guessed that it was April. Jason stepped out behind her. Suzie started to smile at Jason but his serious expression stopped her. The girl that walked towards her looked fragile and young. It was hard for her not to want to comfort her. April brushed past her towards the door. Jason paused beside Suzie and spoke in a low tone.

"I didn't get much out of her. I have no reason to hold her. About the only thing she admitted was knowing Robbie. That's not a reason to arrest her."

"Can't you question her more?"

"Not without cause, Suzie. I did the best I could."

"I know you did, Jason."

As Suzie turned away from him she noticed the door as it swung shut behind April. This was her turn to give it a shot. She hurried after her and caught up with her on the sidewalk in front of the police station.

"April! Wait!"

April turned back and brushed her blonde hair away from her face. "What is it?"

"I'm sorry. I just wanted to ask you a quick question."

"Are you a police officer?"

"No, I'm not. Just curious."

"Curious about what?"

"Did you know Robbie?"

"Look, I said all I was going to say. I have nothing more to add. I don't know why you are harassing me."

"I don't mean to harass you, really I don't. It's just that I have a few questions and it would be so much easier if you answered them. It would be better than your family being questioned about your involvement with Robbie and the thefts at the farm."

April froze and shoved her hands into the pockets of her light jacket. She looked straight at Suzie. "Why are you asking me these questions?"

"April, I just want to help you."

"By threatening to get me in trouble with my family?"

"It's not like that. You're young. There's no way you were the mastermind of all of this. I just want to give you the chance to come clean and maybe not get in as much trouble with the law."

Her lower lip trembled as she closed her eyes. "None of this was supposed to happen."

"What do you mean? What did Robbie get you into?"

"No, it wasn't like that."

"It wasn't? Just tell me the truth, April. We can try to sort it all out."

"Robbie had nothing to do with it."

"What do you mean he had nothing to do with it? He was murdered over it, he had to be involved somehow."

"Not exactly. Look, I don't want to say too much. But Robbie, he was never supposed to get in the middle of any of this."

"Tell me what happened, April."

April pulled her hands out of her pockets and brushed her hands across her face. Suzie noticed some cuts on the skin of her hands.

"Shucking," April said when she noticed that Suzie was looking at them. April curled them into fists to show off the marks. "It's what I do. I shuck the oysters. That's it. All day long. The smell is disgusting. I can't stand it."

"So why do you stay?"

"I have no choice." She sighed. "I'm part of the family. It's the family business."

"Did Robbie have a choice?"

"Robbie was innocent in all of this. I'm not

saying anything else."

"If Robbie wasn't involved then where did he get all of the money from?"

April cringed. "He wasn't involved. He never should have been involved."

"So, you were?" Suzie stared at her. "Were you stealing from your family?"

"It wasn't like that." April closed her eyes and shook her head. "I'm not saying anything else."

"How can I help you if you won't tell me the truth?"

"I can't." She stared up into her eyes. "Don't you see? If I say anything, I'm going to be next. Robbie didn't deserve what happened to him, but I can't do anything about it, he's gone. Now all I can do is worry about protecting myself. I don't have anything else to say."

"If you don't answer the questions the police will have to ask everyone at the farm."

"Then the next time you see me I'll be on a

slab." She shrugged. "Not that it should matter to you."

"It matters to me. If you tell me the truth, I can try to find a way to protect you. I can ask Jason to."

"Tell that to Robbie." She rolled her eyes and skirted past Suzie to the street. "Do what you have to do."

Suzie sighed and stared after her.

"How did I know you wouldn't stay out of this?" Jason's voice carried from just behind her.

"Did you hear all of that?"

"Some."

"Do you think she's telling the truth?"

"I think she's hiding everything."

"But is she hiding it out of fear? Jason, she's so young. What if she gets killed in all of this?"

"Suzie, she's lying to me. There's nothing I can do about it. I'm going to head over to the farm and see what I can find out."

"Wait, Jason. Can you wait until morning?"

"Why would I do that?" He shook his head. "This isn't something I can drag my feet on."

"She seemed scared to me, Jason. She didn't want Robbie to die, something is way off about all of this. I think you should wait a bit before you do anything. At least wait until morning, see if there's any new developments before then."

He sighed and rubbed a hand across his forehead. "It's one day until the wedding, Suzie. It would be much better if I could wrap this up today."

"I know that, Jason, I do. But will you feel like getting married if April shows up dead?"

He frowned. "No. Of course not."

"Then let me follow my instincts."

"What are they telling you?"

"I'm not completely sure, yet. I just want to think this through properly first."

"Okay, but be careful, Suzie. If Robbie really didn't have anything to do with this, then we're dealing with some ruthless killers here."

"I won't do anything. I just want to run it through in my head and it will give you more time to work it out without putting April at risk."

"Okay." He nodded.

"By the way, some of Summer's family are getting in tonight. You should come to Dune House for dinner."

"I don't know, I'm busy with the case."

"Jason. They are going to be your in-laws. It's the respectful thing to do."

Jason laughed and looked over at her. "Are you mothering me?"

"I wouldn't know. But you should have dinner with Summer's family. Right now it might not seem like a big deal, but the impression you leave on them will last."

"Fine. I'll go to dinner." He pointed a finger at

her. "Don't do anything stupid, it's just time to try to work this out."

"I won't." She smiled. On the way to the car she called Paul. "Meet me at the docks. I have a plan."

"I'll be there in five minutes."

Chapter Fifteen

Suzie arrived at the docks just as Paul stepped off his boat.

"Hey, you all right?" He looked into her eyes.

"Why?'

"You look a little shaken."

Suzie smiled at the thought that he could read her so easily. "I'm okay. I want to talk to you about something."

He gestured to a bench beside a low wall that lined the entrance of the dock. "What is it?"

"I think Simon had something to do with this."

"Ah, Suzie, you don't know that."

"No, I don't. But I think that either Robbie or Simon were involved in the thefts from the pearl farm. Or maybe both." She met his eyes. "Do you want to know the truth or do you want to save

203

their reputations?"

"That's not fair, Suzie. Of course I want to know the truth. But I don't want to make unfounded accusations either."

"Paul, please. I know you don't want to believe that Simon could be involved in all of this, but Nina pointed him out in a photograph and identified him as someone who tried to sell her pearls and that wasn't the only time he was in there. What business would Simon have in a jewelry shop? He doesn't seem the type to browse the latest charms and ring settings. So, why was he there?"

"Suzie." He frowned and leaned back against the wall. "It's just that I've known Simon for a long time."

"I know you have, and I know that you don't want to believe that he had anything to do with any of this. But at some point you have to ask yourself whether you are just not facing the truth."

He looked up at her sharply, but the expression faded the moment he met her eyes. "I know you're right." He shook his head. "I just wish that you weren't."

"It's better to know the truth, don't you think, Paul? If we at least find out what really happened to Robbie then you can have some answers for his family. Isn't that what you want?"

"Of course it is. You know better than to question that. But, you're asking me to believe that Simon might have had something to do with Robbie's death. We were all friends."

"You thought you were."

"And if we're wrong? If Simon has nothing to do with any of this? Then I've lost two friends."

"I know that's a risk, but it's not as if we don't have reason to suspect him. He's given us plenty..." She paused and looked into his eyes. "Simon looked me in the eye and threatened me, while you sat right there next to me. That is what I believe. That is what all of the evidence is pointing to."

"Maybe you see it that way, but I need more. I do trust you, Suzie, I do. But I know Simon, and the thought of him hurting Robbie just blows my mind. I need some actual proof that I can't argue with."

"So, let's get it." She folded her arms across her chest. "The best way to find out for sure is to follow him."

"Follow him?"

"Yes. Let's track him. Let's see what he does when no one else is looking. I'm not going to ask you to risk your friendship if I can't prove it to you. So, let's find that proof, one way or the other."

"When do you want to plant a tracker on his boat?"

"Do you have one?"

Paul pursed his lips. He reached into his pocket and pulled out his keys. "Yes. I do."

"Should I ask why?"

"I picked it up earlier today."

Suzie's eyes widened as she waited for further explanation. He sighed and shook his head.

"Maybe I had the same idea you did."

"Seriously?"

"I got it just in case. I thought maybe, if Simon kept acting strange, I'd just see for myself."

"But you weren't going to tell me?"

"It's not because I don't trust you, Suzie. It's because I was trying to be loyal to a friend. But, now I see it's better that we do this together. I'll go grab it."

Suzie watched him hurry off to his car. As she waited for him to return it occurred to her that he had a strong moral code. Even though he suspected his friend, he still did his best to protect him, that was something that she admired.

When he returned, his eyes met hers. "What?"

"Hm?"

"You're smiling."

"Oh, just thinking how lucky I am to be with you."

He shook his head with a short laugh. "Let's get this figured out."

Chapter Sixteen

As Suzie and Paul set off on the boat Suzie kept her attention on the water. It wasn't long before they arrived at Simon's place. His boat was docked, the house up the hill had lights on.

"I think he's home. It'll only take me a second to get this in position. If you see Simon coming, duck down, don't let him know you're here."

"I'll just warn you."

"No." His tone grew firm. "Don't let him know that you're there, if he spots you, this could turn ugly."

"Okay. But you have to be careful, too."

"I can come up with a good explanation for why I'm on the boat. Don't worry."

Suzie nodded, but she did worry, from the moment that he stepped onto the other boat she worried. As she waited for him to return she watched the hill that led up to the house. If there was any sign of Simon, she fully intended to warn Paul. However, he was back on the boat within minutes.

"Okay, it's done." His cheeks flushed.

"It was the right thing, Paul. If nothing comes of it, we'll get the tracker back, and Simon will never know."

"But I'll know." He frowned. Suzie ran her fingertips along the curve of his shoulder until he looked into her eyes.

"It's the right thing, Paul, I promise."

He nodded and eased the boat away from Simon's house. "Now we wait. If he moves, it'll alert us."

The sun began to set as the boat drifted through the water. The tracker remained silent. Suzie began to think that Paul might have been right. All the time she sat there on a quiet boat, in the middle of the ocean, she could be helping Mary with the guests. As a surge of guilt flooded her, the tracker came alive.

"Here, he's on the move." Paul glanced at his watch. "Rather late, too."

"Can you follow him without being spotted?"

"Yes. I can keep a good distance and the tracker will still work. But let's keep it quiet, just in case."

Suzie nodded. Within a few minutes her heart sank. Just as she suspected Simon headed for the pearl farm. He had no reason to go there. He claimed he had no association with them. So why did he stop right at the dock?

"We need to get close, Paul."

"Why?"

"I have a bad feeling. We need to see what he's doing."

"Okay, just keep quiet and still." He turned off the lights on the boat and eased it to a stop not far from the dock. Suzie saw Simon step off his boat onto the dock. There was another figure there, short-statured and hidden by a hoodie. Her skin grew cold as she guessed that it was April. When Simon stepped onto the dock April shied back. His voice carried far enough for them to hear.

"I know you met with the cops today. What did you tell them?"

"Nothing. I didn't tell them anything. I don't even know how they knew to come to me. I don't even know who told them that I knew Robbie."

"Don't worry about that. What did you say to them?"

"Nothing! I wouldn't tell them anything. I can't believe this happened. How could you let this happen?"

"Keep quiet. You have no idea what you're talking about."

"I know that Robbie wasn't in on this!"

"You don't know anything. What happened to Robbie happened. Now, it can either get worse, or we can all walk away from this. So what is it going to be? Do I need to worry about what you might do?"

"No. You don't. I didn't say anything. I won't say anything. But this has to end. It's out of control."

"It's over. Okay?"

"Is it?" Her voice cracked. "I don't think it is."

"It will be. I'll take care of it."

"Is that what you told Robbie?"

"Quiet. Just keep quiet about that."

"Okay, I didn't say anything." She held up her hands and backed away from him.

Simon walked back onto his boat and sped back towards his house. Paul leaned on the railing and closed his eyes.

"I can't believe it. But I have no other choice."

"We don't know everything yet, Paul. But we do know that he was involved, and so was April."

"I need to talk to Simon."

"Paul, no. That's a very bad idea."

"I need to." He looked over at her. "I owe him a face to face conversation."

"No, you don't owe him anything. He's not the man that you thought he was, Paul. Please, let's just go back to the docks."

"You're right." He nodded. "Let's go."

Their ride back to the docks was quiet. Suzie glanced over at him a few times, but his stoic expression made her think that he wasn't up for talking. It didn't seem appropriate for her to say anything. She just lingered close to him and took his hand when she could. When they were close enough Suzie called Jason. There was a lot of noise in the background.

"Hey Suzie, I'm at dinner, like you told me to be."

"Good, that's good. Do you think you can send someone to pick up Simon? We found him at the pearl farm and saw him get into a confrontation with April."

"What? Are you sure?"

"Yes."

"Did he actually put his hands on her?"

"No. But he warned her not to talk to the police."

"I'm not sure that we have enough to pick him up. But we might be able to get a search warrant. Not likely until morning."

"Get it as soon as you can. I'm afraid he might take off. He knows that you spoke to April, so he's spooked."

"All right, I'll see what I can do. But even if we get the warrant that doesn't necessarily mean that we'll find anything," Jason said. "I should have known that you wouldn't stay out of this." He hung up before she could reply.

Paul docked the boat. "I'll catch up with you later."

"Okay, I'm just a phone call away if you want

company," Suzie said as she climbed off the boat.

Paul leaned close to kiss her, then turned to the cabin. Suzie hesitated. She wondered if she should try to stay with him. But Mary had so much on her shoulders with all of the guests that she knew she needed to get back to Dune House.

Chapter Seventeen

By the time Suzie arrived at Dune House, Jason and Summer had already left. Mary was elbow deep in a sink full of dishes.

"Here, let me take over." Suzie stepped up behind her.

"Oh, thank you." Mary yawned. "I could use a sit down." She sat down on one of the kitchen chairs and plopped her feet down on the other.

"How did the dinner go?"

"Fantastic. Everyone got along well, and Summer was so pleased that Jason was here."

"I'm glad he was, too."

"Now, what about you? Jason mentioned something about you going off on an adventure and never listening."

"Something like that." Suzie frowned as she ran a sponge across a plate. "Paul and I followed Simon."

"You did? What did you find out?"

"I'm pretty sure he was involved in the thefts at the pearl farm and maybe even Robbie's death."

"Wow. How did Paul take it?"

"It's hard to say with Paul. Sometimes he's hard to read. I know that it's bothering him."

"Is Jason arresting Simon?"

"Not yet, he said that he wouldn't even be able to get a search warrant until morning."

"Ugh, that is cutting it close to the wedding."

"I know, but it's procedure." Suzie frowned. "I just hope that Simon doesn't take off before Jason has a chance to arrest him. It would have been so nice if all of this was done and taken care of today."

"Yes, it would. Too bad for Paul though."

"It is. I think he's starting to realize his friendship with Simon wasn't what he thought it was."

"Better to know, I suppose."

"I just hope he doesn't feel like I'm attacking him."

"I'm sure he doesn't. You have to trust him a little, to know your heart."

"You're right." She finished the dishes and turned around to face her. "So, what's on the agenda for the morning?"

"I've offered everyone breakfast, but they've made arrangements to have breakfast at that cute little café on the water. So it should be pretty quiet here in the morning."

"Oh good, that will give us some time to go over what still needs to be done for the wedding."

"Actually, we're pretty good on that. The centerpieces are done, the decorations are ready to go up, I double-checked on the reservations for the chairs, and I double checked the new order of shellfish with the fisherman that Paul recommended."

"Wonderful. You are amazing, Mary."

"Really? I'm not the one solving a murder."

"No, you're the one pulling off the perfect wedding for two very busy people while your best friend, who you should be able to rely on, is off running around town."

"Suzie, I know that I can always rely on you. Don't ever think that I don't."

Suzie hugged her and smiled. "Ditto Mary. I guess we'd both better get some sleep and hope that everything goes smoothly over the next couple of days."

"Good idea." Mary stretched and yawned again. "I've got the calls forwarded to my room if any of the guests need anything."

"Okay, if there's any crisis, feel free to wake me up."

"You'll be the first to know." Mary laughed and headed to her room.

Once Suzie was in bed she tried to sleep, but

her mind was too revved up with what she saw that night. If Simon hurt Robbie, would he hurt April, too? The thought of the young woman being harmed made her restless. At some point she fell asleep because her cell phone woke her up early the next morning.

"Hello?" She mumbled into the phone.

"Suzie, it's Jason. I got that search warrant, but there's a problem."

"What?"

"We went to Simon's place and he isn't there. It looks like he might have cleaned some things out so he can take off."

"Oh no." She sighed.

"I'll update you if anything happens, but I just wanted you and Paul to be on the lookout."

"Thanks for the heads up, Jason. I'll let Paul know."

She hung up the phone and dragged herself to her feet. It seemed to her that she hadn't slept at all. She met Mary in the kitchen just as she set up a pot of coffee.

"Mm, perfect timing." Suzie smiled. She called Paul's number as she waited for the coffee to brew. Paul didn't answer. She sent him a text. Again, he didn't respond. Paul was always up earlier than her. If the sun was up Paul was up and often long before the sun was up, he was up. So, why wasn't he answering? Her heart started to race. What if Simon confronted Paul? Or the other way around?

"Here Suzie." Mary handed her a cup of coffee.

"No, no thank you. I have to go."

"What? What's wrong?"

"I think Paul might be in trouble."

"Then I'll come with you. All of the guests are out and Summer is with them, I gave her a spare key in case she needed to organize something for the wedding and we weren't available. I'll call her on the way so she knows that they can call me if they need anything. We'll go find Paul."

"Are you sure?"

"Absolutely. Here, I'll pop some coffee into a thermos. Then Paul can have some, too."

Two minutes later they headed out the door towards the docks.

Chapter Eighteen

As Suzie drove with Mary towards the docks her heart raced even faster. Nightmare scenarios played through her mind. Sure, she was overreacting, but for some reason she couldn't stop it. She parked and jumped out of the car. Suzie surveyed the boats at the dock. She looked twice before she admitted to herself that Paul's boat wasn't there.

"Mary, something's not right. Paul must have taken the boat out without telling me."

"Do you think he would do that?" Mary frowned. "Maybe he went to Simon himself?'

"Oh no, I hope not. If Paul goes to Simon and hints that he knows he was involved somehow, then he could be in grave danger. We have to go after him."

"But how? We can't just go out on a boat ourselves."

"No, we're going to need some help." Suzie looked over at Mike's boat. She noticed him near the edge of the boat. He tried hard to pretend that he wasn't looking at them. "Mike!" She strode towards him with as much confidence as she could muster. "I need your help."

"I don't want to be involved." He turned his back to her.

"Mike, please. Paul's life might be in danger. I'm sorry that we suspected you, but now I know that you weren't involved. But there's only one way to prove it. Right now you're still a suspect. You have no alibi, you have a history of conflict with Robbie. But we need to prove who did do it so you can stop being on the suspect list."

He sighed and turned back to face her. "How do I know this isn't some trick?"

"If I really thought that you were a murderer do you think I would ask you to help me and my best friend? Do you think I would ever put her in that kind of danger?"

Mike looked past her to Mary, who stood a few feet behind Suzie. Mary held up a hand and waved a little. "I'm the best friend. Trust me, she is very overprotective."

He shook his head again. "Fine, you don't suspect me, but it sounds to me that you're trying to get yourself tangled up in something very dangerous, and that's not something I want to be involved in. Why would I put my life at risk, my boat at risk?"

"It's Paul, Mike. You two have been on these docks together for a long time."

"And maybe if he had listened to me from the beginning none of this would have happened. He wanted to believe that Robbie was so innocent, I tried to warn him to not get into someone else's business, but he didn't want to hear me. He also suspected me and I might not be the most liked fisherman around here, but I am trustworthy, and Paul should have known that."

Mary met his eyes. "Mike, he did. If you were

in trouble you know that Paul would have helped you. Are you really going to put Paul's life at risk, all because you want to make a point?"

He frowned. "I try to follow a policy of staying out of business that has nothing to do with me. But you're right. I don't want the police to keep sniffing around me. Eventually they'll find something to pin on me. So I will take you out, but the first sign of trouble, we are turning back."

"Absolutely." Suzie smiled. "Thank you, Mike."

Mike clenched his jaw and reached his hand out to her to help her onto the boat. Then he reached out to Mary. As Suzie saw Mike grab hold of Mary's hand she wondered if she'd made the right choice.

"Are you sure you're okay to go out on the water?" Suzie asked Mary.

Mary nodded yes. She didn't like being on a boat nearly as much as Suzie, but she was getting used to them and she couldn't let Suzie go out there alone.

A jolt of fear shot through Suzie as the possibility that she was wrong about Mike played through her mind. But it was too late to change her mind. The engine roared and the boat lurched away from the dock.

Mary clung to the railing so tightly that her knuckles turned white. She looked out over the water. Suzie moved into place right beside her. She scanned the horizon. Maybe she would spot Paul's boat. Maybe he hadn't gotten as much of a head start as they expected he did. However, the wide open ocean was empty. Not only was Paul's boat not there, she didn't see any other boats on the water either.

"So, where are we headed?" Mike looked over at her with a scowl. "I need to make this fast, I have other things to do."

"To Simon's place."

"Simon?" Mike raised an eyebrow. "Why?"

"Because I think that's where Paul went. They're friends."

"So, why are we chasing him down there? He would be safe with Simon."

"Just go to Simon's place, please." Suzie met his eyes. Mike stared at her for a moment, then set his course. She guessed that he had more questions, but she didn't want to answer them. Until she knew for sure that her suspicions were true she didn't want to sully Simon's name. Was that even where Paul went? She didn't know. Above them the sky rumbled. Suzie looked at Mary and noticed how pale she was.

"We can't stay out here long. The storm is coming our way." Mike narrowed his eyes. "I'll take you to Paul, then I'm heading back. Understand? I can't risk my boat."

"I understand." Suzie nodded. As Mike's boat approached Simon's place she noticed Paul's boat at the dock. A sense of relief and terror flooded her. Relief that Paul was there, but terror that

Simon might have done something to hurt him. "Look Mary. Do you see Paul on the boat?"

Mary leaned forward over the railing and shook her head. "No, I don't see anyone on there."

"What will it be ladies, am I leaving you here, or taking you back with me?" Mike looked at them both with taut lips, then up at the dark sky. "There's very little time left to get back to the docks."

"Mary, why don't you go back with him? You can check on Jason and Summer while I ride back with Paul."

Mary's hand closed over Suzie's. She met Suzie's eyes. "I'm not going anywhere without you, Suzie. If you're getting off this boat, so am I."

Suzie nodded and looked over at Mike. "I guess we're both getting off here."

He hesitated and looked at the sky again. "Are you sure? This looks pretty nasty."

"We'll be fine." Suzie swung her leg over the

side of the boat. Mike stepped up to help her over, then helped Mary as well. As the boat lurched away from the dock Mike called out to them again.

"Don't let Paul get on the water in this. You three hunker down with Simon. He'll take care of you."

Suzie grimaced at the thought, but she waved to Mike as he turned the boat around. Briefly she considered calling him back, but that ship had sailed. She turned back to Simon's house. The property was as littered with debris as it had been when she had visited before, but somehow in the eerie glow of the storm that approached everything appeared dangerous. Was the mess evidence of a murderous mind? Had she overlooked clear signs that Simon was a danger to Paul? She pushed the thoughts down and walked beside Mary up the hill towards the small house. This time there was no delicious smell coming from the kitchen. In fact, like Jason had said it didn't seem to her that anyone was home. It struck her then that Simon's boat was not there.

"Oh no!" Suzie turned back towards the small dock. "Paul must have gone on Simon's boat with him."

"You're right, they're not here." Mary turned away from the window she'd peered through. "There's no one inside."

"That means Simon could have taken him anywhere. And in this storm. We have to find them!"

"Maybe we should call Jason, I bet he has a way to track the boat." Mary pulled out her phone.

"That's it!" Suzie snapped her fingers. "Mary, you're a genius."

"What?" Mary's finger hovered above the keypad.

"Yesterday Paul and I put a tracking device on Simon's boat. That's how we discovered that he went out to the pearl farm in the middle of the night. I bet it's still active. As long as the feed is live we can track Simon's boat from Paul's."

"That's great, Suzie, but we don't have a captain." Mary shook her head. "How are we going to track them if they're traveling on water?"

"We have no other choice. We're going to have to try. Paul has shown me enough to handle the boat in case of an emergency."

"Well, this is certainly an emergency." Mary followed Suzie down towards the dock. Just as they reached the boat a clap of thunder made them both jump. It was not the type of storm that anyone should be headed out to sea in, especially Suzie and Mary, who had about as much experience with boats as a guest on a cruise ship. Suzie paused and looked over at Mary.

"You should stay here. Call Jason. Tell him what's happening and to send a boat out to pick you up."

"No Suzie, I'm not going to do that."

"What if they come back? Someone will need

to be here to explain why Paul's boat is missing."

Mary narrowed her eyes. She stepped onto the boat. "You are not going out into those rough waters without me, Suzie. We are in this together, just like everything else we've ever been through."

Suzie smiled at her and offered a quick hug before heading for the controls. As much as she wanted Mary to be safe, it was a relief to know that she always had her back. As the boat sped off across the water Suzie did her best to remain in control of it. Mary held on to the tracking device. But the waves grew bigger, and the boat lurched from side to side.

"Can you tell where they are, Mary?"

"Not far, Suzie. Just keep going. Not far."

It wasn't long before Suzie recognized the path they took. They were headed straight for the pearl farm.

"Why are they going out there?" Her breath caught in her throat. Was Simon taking him out there to hurt him? She stared so hard at the water ahead of her that her eyes stung. Simon's boat had to be somewhere. As she suspected it was right beside the dock at the pearl farm.

"There!" Suzie pointed to it. "Let's get close."

"All right. But I don't see anyone on the boat, Suzie."

As soon as they were close enough Suzie climbed off the boat and onto the dock. She peered into Simon's boat. "Paul?"

"Is he there, Suzie?"

"He must be in the cabin." Suzie's heart lurched. If Paul wasn't answering her there had to be a reason. She boarded the boat and walked through it. "No, no, it's empty." Suzie cringed as she looked through the boat one more time. The only thing that gave her any comfort was the fact that there was no evidence of a fight onboard the boat.

"Then they must be somewhere on the land."

Mary scanned the horizon. "Is there even anything out here?"

"Yes, there's a house about a mile in. We're going to have to hike. Are you up for it?" Suzie frowned with concern. Mary nodded and straightened her shoulders.

"I can handle it."

As they began down the path towards the house Suzie watched for any sign of the direction that Paul and Simon took. Was Paul his hostage? Did Simon convince him that he was innocent? If so, what were they doing at the pearl farm? About halfway to the house, Suzie heard a sound in the distance. It sounded like the slam of a car door. They were far from the driveway and any road. But obviously there was a vehicle nearby.

"Mary, did you hear that?"

"Yes. I think it came from over there." She pointed to a low hill not far from where they stood.

"Sh." Suzie put her finger to her lips then began walking in the direction of the hill. Mary walked right behind her. "I think there's a car over there. Do you see it?"

"I think so." Mary peered through the brush. "Is that even a road?"

"Whether it is or not, they've turned it into one."

"Do you think Paul is in the car?"

"I'm not sure. But I'm going to find out. You stay here." She turned to look at Mary.

"Suzie, I said I would stick with you and I meant it."

"Mary, if something goes wrong and I end up in danger, I'm going to need you to get help. You're the only one that knows what's going on here. If I'm not back in ten minutes, go back to Paul's boat and use the radio to call Jason for help. Okay?"

"No, it's not okay." Mary frowned. "What if

something happens to you?"

"I will be fine, I promise. I need to know that you can call for help if we need it. Will you do that?"

"Yes, I will." Mary's hands balled into fists at her sides. "But I don't like this. Not at all."

"I know that." She looked through the brush again, then back at Mary. "Everything will be fine. Remember, we have a wedding to host."

"Yes, a wedding." She nodded. "So make sure you don't get hurt."

"Don't worry."

Chapter Nineteen

Suzie slipped through the brush towards the car. She could hear muffled voices but couldn't make out what they were saying. Then she heard Paul's familiar voice.

"This is crazy. You are not going to get away with this."

"But I already have. No one knows that you're here, do they?"

"Look, there has to be a reasonable way that we can work this out."

"No, there's really not." Suzie crept a few steps forward in an attempt to get a good look at the man she heard. However, when she set her foot down, she shattered a shell beneath her shoe. The sound drew the attention of an armed man. She couldn't make out who he was, but he was headed straight towards her. Suzie's breath caught in her throat when she saw the man who held the gun.

Pedro.

"Well, look who it is?" Pedro pointed the gun at her. She held her breath. Even with her panicked mind she remembered the cut on his hand and the oyster shells in his trashcan and in that moment she could think of a thousand ways that she could have avoided exposing herself to him. However, it was too late for that. She looked past Pedro, at Paul, who grimaced the moment he saw her. "Your girlfriend is here?" Pedro smirked at Paul. "Time for a party." Pedro moved his gun from Suzie and pointed it at Paul. "Hm?"

"Leave her alone!" Paul demanded sharply.

"Looks like I can handle everyone at once. Come on." He waved his gun at Suzie to move her in the direction of the door.

Suzie's eyes widened when she saw Simon stagger to his feet as Pedro pointed the gun at him. Simon kept his eyes to the ground. Was he even involved in this? Pedro ushered them towards a path.

"Let them go, they didn't have anything to do with this," Simon said.

"Sure. I'll just let you all walk away, now that you know that I'm involved. Move it." He shoved Simon forward. Paul looked over at her with wide eyes as if he might lunge for the gun, but she shook her head slightly. It was too risky. She held her breath as they walked past the area where Mary was a few moments before. Luckily there was no sign of her. Pedro led the three of them back to Simon's boat and ordered them on board. Suzie tried to convince herself that he would be merciful and let them go, but she knew that there wasn't much chance of that.

"Go inside." Pedro waved the gun in their direction.

"Why? What are you going to do?" Paul started to move towards Suzie, but Pedro held him back. "Get inside." He released the safety on the weapon. "Don't move, or you're not going to live to take another breath."

Simon walked into the cabin. Pedro shoved Paul in. Suzie followed close behind.

"Against the wall." He gestured with the gun towards the back wall of Simon's boat. Simon didn't argue. When Paul stood still and didn't move he aimed the gun at Suzie's head. "Up against the wall, Paul! Or she gets it." Paul went against the wall next to Simon.

"What are you going to do to us?" Suzie stared at Pedro and kept her feet planted exactly where she was.

"Do as I say." Pedro gestured to the wall again. "Oh no, Simon's about to be held responsible for another murder." He grimaced.

Suzie regulated the pattern of her breaths in an attempt to avoid panic. She suspected that the moment her back hit the wall the man would pull the trigger and they would all be killed, and he planned to frame Simon for their murders. She thought of Mary and wondered if she would be able to get help. Outside the boat she heard a loud roll of thunder. Rain pelted the boat and the rough water around it. With the storm that raged no helicopter or boat would be able to reach them anytime soon.

"Not unless you tell me what is going on here. What are you going to do?" She looked into Pedro's eyes. They were cold and indicated that he had no desire to sympathize with her. However, he lowered the weapon a few inches. "These are the people you have known for years. They are your friends. Robbie was a fisherman and just a young man."

"I don't care. I don't care about any of that. Robbie was not one of us, he was a coward and he is a part of my past. You're all going to be just a part of my past. So close your mouth and do as I say."

"Why would you kill us? You could just let us go. Are you really going to shoot all three of us?" Suzie asked.

"Shoot? No. I don't need any more drama

again." Pedro smirked. "The storm can do my dirty work for me."

"Why are you doing this?" Suzie asked. "Did you kill Robbie?" She wanted to keep him talking and she wanted a full confession.

"Enough!" Pedro said harshly. He reached down and threw some ropes to Paul and Simon. "Tie them up, around the railing." He gestured to Suzie.

"But we'll never survive out there on the water," Suzie said.

"Exactly." He aimed the gun at Suzie. She bent down and tied the ropes around Simon's hands, her hands were trembling. Then she tied them around Paul's. She tried to keep them loose. Pedro gestured to the wall. "Now, against the wall."

She backed up against the wall next to Paul. She moved closer to him.

"Stop!" Pedro shouted. "Stay exactly where

you are." Suzie stopped. Maybe the illusion of compliance would keep her alive long enough to form a plan. If Pedro didn't plan to shoot them they had a better chance of survival. But what were the chances with the storm that thrashed the water around the boat?

The boat started moving more violently as the storm picked up. She wondered if she might be able to use that to her advantage. Pedro trained his gun on her. She needed a way out. Maybe if she could distract him she could get the gun away from him.

"Oh, I'm feeling so sick." She pressed her hand against her stomach. "I can't help it, I think I'm going to vomit. Can I go to the bathroom?"

"Stay right there."

She groaned and made a choking sound in her throat. "Ugh, I'm going to be sick." She coughed and gurgled.

"Shut up!" He grimaced as there was a loud crash of thunder and the boat lurched to the side.

All of a sudden she saw her opportunity and lunged forward. She reached for the wrist of the hand that held the gun in the same moment that she drove her shoulder into his chest. However, Pedro was much stronger than she expected and more used to the rolling seas. He wobbled a little, but did not tumble. The force did knock the gun out of his hand. When it fell to the floor of the boat a shot rang out. Suzie froze. Had she been hit? Had Paul or Simon been hit?

After a moment passed and no one cried out in pain and she could feel no searing pain anywhere in her body Suzie dove for the weapon. Pedro dove for it at the same time. She managed to snatch it up before he did. The boat rocked so hard that Suzie rolled to the other side of the boat. She almost lost her footing. She gripped the gun as tight as she could. Water spurted through the hole that the stray bullet had left in the boat. Pedro also fell with the lurch of the boat. He crawled towards the door. She rushed up to him and lifted the butt of the gun prepared to slam it down on his head and knock him out, but before she could he swept his leg through her legs and she crashed to the floor. As she did she lost the grip on the gun and Pedro snatched it off the ground and shoved it in her face as he got to his feet. Suzie shuddered at the sound of a crash of thunder.

"Nice try." He smirked. "Now against the wall!" He shouted. She stood up and walked towards the wall.

"Suzie." Paul frowned. "Are you okay?"

"I am. Are you?" She looked into his eyes.

He nodded and glanced over at Pedro. "Just let us go. There's no reason to make this worse."

"Oh, I'm going to let you go all right. I'm just going to tie Suzie up." He grabbed a length of rope and tied her hands up. She hoped that if she didn't fight he wouldn't bother to tie the rope too tight, but she was wrong. He tied it so tight that it cut into her wrists. She bit into her bottom lip to keep from crying out.

Pedro checked Paul and Simon's ropes and tightened them. Once they were all tightly tied up, Pedro headed towards the cabin door.

"Pedro." Simon spoke for the first time. "Don't let them die this way."

"Ha Ha, acting innocent now," Pedro said. "If you didn't stuff up and get caught by Robbie then we wouldn't be in this mess and Robbie would be alive."

"You can kill me, but please let them go," Simon pleaded. As Suzie listened to the conversation she tried to make sense of what they were saying. Was he trying to save them? Was Simon innocent?

"Good luck." Pedro chuckled as he pulled the cabin door shut. Suzie heard something slide into place to block them in. As her heart raced she looked over at Paul.

"What are our chances?"

He looked into her eyes. "It's you and me,

darling. There's no chance we won't get out of this. Turn your back to mine, I'll get you untied." He stretched out his hands towards her, but the fact that they were tied around the railing restricted his movement. She did as he instructed while she kept a watchful eye on Simon in the corner. His rough fingertips scraped along her palm and wrists as he tugged at the ropes around her wrists. She winced as the harder he tugged the tighter they became.

"Paul, it's not working. It's not working." She pulled her hands away from him. "You're making it tighter."

"I'm sorry without being able to see it's really hard to do."

"Let me help." Simon stood up from the corner. His hands were untied and in one hand he held a knife.

"How did you get out of the rope, Simon?" Suzie shied back as he approached her.

"I had a knife in my pocket. Pedro didn't find

it because I keep it tucked behind my cigarette pack. It throws off the cops, too." He held the knife out towards her. "Let me get you free."

"Don't come near me." She glared at him.

"Suzie, it's okay," Paul said.

"It's not, Paul. He's the one that caused all of this. He's the one that killed Robbie."

"He didn't." Paul frowned. "Pedro did and now, we're all in the same boat, literally. Simon's not going to hurt you."

"I wish I could believe that."

"Let me show you." Simon lowered the knife but stepped towards her. "I'm not going to hurt you, Suzie. I know what you must think of me, and you're not wrong. I did a horrible thing. I kept his murderer a secret. I did try to save him. If I wasn't involved he might never have been murdered. But I'm not going to make the same mistake again, I'm not going to let someone else die. If we're going to survive this storm we're all going to have to work together."

Suzie's stomach churned at the thought of working with someone that was involved in a murder. She glanced over at Paul who nodded to her. With a deep sigh she turned her back to Simon. With every step he took towards her she waited for the plunge of the knife into her back. However, all she felt was the cool glide of the blade against her wrist as he slipped it between her skin and the tight ropes around it. With one sharp movement he cut her free. Her eyes filled with tears as the pain in her wrists finally eased. She rubbed them and turned back to face him.

"Give me the knife." She held out her hand to him.

"What? I can free Paul."

"No. You're not going anywhere near him with that knife. Give it to me and I will cut him loose."

"What if you decide to kill me first?" Simon stared at her.

"Of the two of us, who has more chance of doing that?" She glared into his eyes. Simon frowned and glanced over at Paul.

"You weren't lying about her courage."

"Give her the knife, Simon. This boat is going down fast." Paul looked towards the water that reached up to his ankles. Simon handed her the knife. Suzie hurried over to Paul and cut his hands free. Then she tucked the knife into her back pocket. There was no time to argue or even discuss their escape. The boat lurched hard to the left, then to the right, and a huge wave of water washed into the cabin. She shoved her shoulder against the door in an attempt to open it, but it wouldn't budge.

"We're not going to get out this way," Suzie said.

"Simon, grab that ax!" Paul pointed to an ax that hung on a wall among other tools. "We're going to hack our way out."

"Good idea." Simon grabbed the ax and tossed

it to Paul. Paul swung it hard at the door. He continued to swing, harder and harder, until finally the door splintered open. He made enough of an opening to get through.

"Stay close. This boat might roll." Paul grabbed her hand and guided her out in front of him. As soon as Suzie was outside she was hit with a deluge of rain. She tried to see past it, but it was impossible. Paul and Simon climbed out onto the deck after her. Just as they made it out, the boat surged hard to the right, and Suzie lost all sense of direction as she flew up into the air.

Chapter Twenty

Mary pulled herself to her feet, but the slippery deck of Paul's boat made it nearly impossible to keep her footing. She wrapped her arms around the railing and clung tight. She peered through the driving rain in the direction of the last place that she saw Simon's boat. However, all she could make out were rolling waves. She saw no sign of the boat. Her heart dropped into the pit of her stomach. Where was Suzie? All of her seasickness left her as she was sick with worry.

"Suzie!" She screamed her name, but the roar of the wind ripped it away. She'd never experienced anything more frustrating than screaming without making much of a sound. She rushed back to the radio again and grabbed it. She hadn't been able to hear a response from anyone. She had no idea if anyone was on the way.

"Jason, are you out there? Jason?"

The crackle that returned over the radio had a

hint of a voice. She squeezed the radio in her hand. "Jason, please. I'm on Paul's boat. We're out on the water. Simon's boat is gone, we need help out here! At the pearl farm!"

Again the radio crackled. She still couldn't make out what was said. To her relief the rain began to let up. It seemed to her that the wind pushed the boat far from the last place she'd seen Simon's boat. Seconds later flashing lights in the distance drew her attention. She recognized the police boat and yelled as loud as she could.

"Jason!" Mary waved furiously to him from the boat. "Jason!"

The police boat drifted close to Paul's. "Mary, are you okay? Where are Suzie and Paul?"

"I don't know. I've been searching for them. They were trapped on Simon's boat. I tried to get to them, but the storm kept pushing me away. Jason, I'm afraid something terrible has happened."

Jason shaded his eyes as he looked over the

water. "Knowing my cousin, she is just fine. Look. Maybe they are there, I think I see some movement." He looked through his binoculars and pointed to a small scrap of land that couldn't even be called an island. "I bet they're over there. Let's go take a look." He offered her a hand to help her onto his boat. One of the patrol officers climbed onto Paul's boat.

"Take it back to the docks, but don't let anyone else touch it. Understand?"

"Yes sir." He nodded as he took control of Paul's boat. Mary clung to the sides of the seat she perched on.

"Please hurry, Jason. This storm is terrible."

Jason headed for the piece of land. "Keep an eye out, Mary, if you see anyone in the water let me know."

"I'm looking." Mary's voice wavered with fear. She leaned so far forward that she could feel the spray from the water as the boat ploughed through it. Fresh tears flooded her eyes which made it hard for her to see. She blinked them back and stared hard at the water. By the time they reached the land the tears fell freely down her cheeks.

"Are they there? Do you see them?" Jason grimaced and pulled out a pair of binoculars. He scanned as much of the land as he could see. Just when he was going to put the binoculars away he saw a big piece of cloth. It flapped in the wind that still blew hard across the water.

"Suzie?" He shouted and climbed off the boat. Mary followed after him and scrambled to get from the water to the sand.

"Do you see her? Where is she? Suzie! Paul!"

"Here!" Suzie's voice carried across the sand. Mary's heart raced with joy. Suzie pushed herself to her feet and waved her arms above her head. "We're here!"

Jason jogged up to her. "Are you hurt?" He looked her over.

"No, I'm okay. But Paul, and Simon." She gestured to the two men on the sand beside her.

"Paul!" Jason dropped down beside him. "Can you hear me?"

"I can." Paul's voice shook as he spoke. "I'm okay, just a little tired."

Jason began to assess his vitals. Mary threw her arms around Suzie. "I'm so sorry I couldn't get to you. I tried so hard."

"You stayed with me, Mary." Suzie hugged her back as she peered over her shoulder at Paul who managed to sit up. "I heard you the entire time. Your voice kept me going. We made it to land, and I knew that you would be sending help."

"Jason, don't fuss over me, I'm fine." Paul waved him away, though his skin was pale and his lips tinted blue. "I swallowed a bit too much sea water that's all. I'll be fine once it settles."

"They can check that out at the hospital." Jason looked him hard in the eyes. "No argument."

"No argument." Paul held up his hands. He looked over at Simon who was still lying on the sand as a police officer administered mouth to mouth. "I had to knock him out. He fought me when I tried to pull him out of the water. I don't know how much water he took in. He was stealing pearls from the farm with Pedro, but Pedro killed Robbie. Pedro is the murderer. You have to get him."

"Don't worry about that now. We'll get him. Let's just get you home." Jason looked over Simon and nodded. "He's still alive. I'll get some back-up." As Jason spoke into his radio Suzie pulled away from Mary and wrapped her arms around Paul. She kissed his forehead and cheek.

"I'm so glad that you're okay," Paul said.

"Me, too." Suzie patted his back and shook her head.

"You two gave me such a scare. I'm getting too old for this you know," Mary said.

"The way you handled my boat told a different story. I'm amazed that you were able to keep it afloat in that storm. If you hadn't, who knows what might have happened."

"Let's not think about that now." Suzie sighed and closed her eyes as she held onto him. "We made it. That's all I want to think about."

A wave of relief, larger than any the storm had carved from the sea gave her such a deep sense of comfort that tears flooded her eyes. She wanted nothing more than to remain there in his grasp, but the police would have questions, and the wedding needed to go on. She reluctantly pulled away and looked into both Paul and Mary's faces in turn.

"I love you both so much. Thank you for being here for me."

"We were here for each other." Mary smiled between them. "Like we always will be."

Chapter Twenty-One

Once Paul was cleared by the doctors he went back to Dune House with Suzie. At the bed and breakfast Suzie, Mary, and Paul huddled around the kitchen table. Summer poured them each a cup of tea, then joined them. Jason spoke on his cell phone a few feet away.

"What I don't understand is, why would Pedro kill Robbie if they were in on the thefts together?" Suzie frowned.

"That's not what happened. Robbie had no idea what Simon was doing. Simon said that he was taking tourists out for night trips and asked to use Robbie's boat because it was new. He gave him part of the earnings," Paul said.

"That's where Robbie got all of the money from." Suzie shook her head.

"Yes, only Simon was not taking tourists out. He was working with Pedro to steal pearls from the pearl farm. April alerted them when it was a suitable time, because they promised her she would get a share. She wanted to get away from her family. She met Simon through Pedro, and Simon got involved, too. But Robbie never did."

"So, Robbie was innocent," Suzie smiled.

"Yes, it seems that way."

"Robbie was becoming suspicious about what Simon was doing and started asking questions so Simon got worried. Robbie asked him if he could go out for the night trip with him on the day he was murdered. Simon said yes, but he sabotaged Robbie's boat because if the boat was giving trouble then Simon had an excuse not to take it out that night without making Robbie more suspicious."

"Wow, complicated but clever," Suzie said. "But the mechanic fixed it."

"Simon thought that Robbie would call the regular mechanic who he knew was away so he thought he would have to wait, but Robbie got Gill to look at it and it was fixed quickly."

"Why did Pedro kill Robbie?" Suzie asked.

"I'm getting there," Paul said. "Simon had stashed the pearls on Robbie's boat because the dock was busy. He knew that the boat was fixed because Simon gave Gill a lift back. After he had dropped off Gill, Simon knew that he had to get the pearls and sabotage Robbie's boat again, so he couldn't take the boat out and it would just look like Gill hadn't fixed it properly. He wore a yellow jacket to look like Gill so if anyone saw him and told Robbie, he would think that it was still Gill on his boat. But it all went wrong when Robbie came back to the boat and caught Simon getting the pearls he had stashed. Robbie then knew about the thefts at the pearl farm and he knew exactly what Simon had done."

"Was he going to turn him in?" Suzie asked.

"No, according to Simon he wasn't as long as they stopped. Simon was happy to take Robbie's word that he would keep quiet. But Pedro came back to the boat and he didn't trust that Robbie would keep his mouth shut and he didn't want to give up on the money from the pearls they were stealing. Simon tried to reason with Pedro, but Pedro took the oyster shucker from the table and stabbed Robbie to get rid of the problem."

"How terrible." Suzie stared hard at the table. "This entire time I've suspected Robbie and the truth was he was killed by a fellow fisherman, all because of money."

"Simon said he wanted to protect him and he tried to help Robbie. That's how he got blood on the jacket. But he was scared of going to jail and scared that Pedro would kill him if he told the police what had happened."

"Why did you go to the pearl farm with Simon?" Suzie asked.

"Simon was worried that Pedro was going to hurt April to keep her quiet so we went there to protect her," Paul said.

"Just awful." Mary clutched her cup of tea.

"The important thing is that the murder is solved, and everyone is safe." Paul looked around the table at the group as Jason hung up his phone and joined them. "That never would have happened without all of us working together."

"He's right." Jason nodded. "If we dwell on what could have happened we won't be able to move forward." He looked over at Summer and smiled. He was distracted by the ring of his cell phone again. He walked away to answer it. As Suzie watched she saw his muscles relax. He strode back towards them with a smile on his face after he had hung up. "Good news. Pedro has just been arrested."

"That is good. We can put this all behind us," Paul said solemnly.

"I think we've weathered this storm pretty well," Jason said.

"Yes, we have," Summer said. "We can always have the wedding another day."

"What?" Suzie shook her head. "Absolutely

not. The wedding must go on."

"Oh Suzie, don't you want to rest and recover from all of this? Do you really think you'll be up for it?" Summer said.

"Sweetheart, one of the main reasons I fought so hard was because I had this wedding to look forward to. Mary and I can get everything set up at Dune House. Your family and friends that flew from out-of-town are already settled here. Everything will be just fine, Summer. Unless you two really want to postpone, it is your day."

"I don't." Jason looked into Summer's eyes. "The last thing I want is to go another day without being married to you. Do you think we can still do this?"

Summer smiled and gave his hand a squeeze. "I feel the same way, Jason. If everyone is still willing, then I am more than happy to go through with it."

"Wonderful." Suzie smiled with relief. "I can't wait. Mary, you and I have some work to do."

"Let's get to it." Mary stood up. "As for you two, early to bed, and plenty of rest, hm?" She looked between Summer and Jason.

"Yes ma'am." Jason smiled and stood up as well.

By the time the last of the pre-wedding preparations were completed, Suzie was exhausted. It was hard to believe that she'd survived a storm on the ocean that morning, and had a hand in a killer being arrested. She collapsed into bed, ready to sleep forever. Yet again she closed her eyes for what felt like five minutes, when she opened them again the sun glared through the window. Her heart raced. Did she oversleep? A quick glance at the clock reassured her that she woke up right on time.

The scent of coffee and pancakes alerted her to the fact that Mary was already up and cooking breakfast for their guests. Since the wedding was in the afternoon they had offered to host a brunch for the out-of-town guests. Suzie climbed out of bed and swayed. For a moment it seemed as if she was back on the boat. As she regained her balance a surge of gratitude washed over her. What she had survived the day before was nothing short of amazing. The thought of not being able to be there for the wedding had made her determined to get through. It had all turned out well, but she wasn't naive enough not to recognize just how lucky she was. She dressed and met Mary in the kitchen.

"What can I help with?"

"Pancakes need flipping!" She tossed her the spatula. Suzie caught it and began flipping the pancakes. Being side by side with Mary was the most natural position that she could imagine. Not long ago she didn't even realize she was lonely, now her life was filled with warmth, excitement, and love. As the guests made their way down into the kitchen everyone buzzed with conversation about the wedding. Suzie excused herself to make some last minute phone calls to confirm things for the wedding.

Once outside on the deck where it was a bit quieter she spotted the chairs and archway being set up on the sand. The beach would be a perfect backdrop for the wedding photographs. Despite the chaos that had led up to the day of the wedding, everything had fallen into place quite nicely. After confirming with vendors and the bakery that all deliveries would be made on time Suzie stretched her arms above her head and took a deep breath of the sea air.

"Gorgeous."

She turned with a smile at the sound of Paul's voice. When she met his eyes he wrapped his arms around her. "I almost didn't want to say a word, but you were too beautiful to resist."

"Hm, sounds like you're getting into a romantic mood from all this wedding chatter."

"I'm just so glad that you're here to hold, that I'm here to hold you. That close call yesterday reminded me of just how lucky I am." He brushed his palm along her cheek. "I hope that you feel the

269

same way about me."

"I do." She kissed him lightly on the lips. "I am very lucky. My life has changed so much, and never once could I have imagined that moving here would turn out to be such an adventure."

"I wish you had never been in any danger, Suzie, but I'm glad that we were there for each other when we needed each other."

"Me too, Paul." She tightened her arms around his waist. "If there is ever any trouble that we face, I know that we will be able to handle it together. The only other person I've trusted that much is Mary."

"Then I'm honored to be included in that small group." He smiled. "I think I'm going to make a captain out of her yet."

"If you can get her back out on a boat after yesterday, I'll believe in miracles."

"That will make two of us."

***

As the ceremony started Paul led Suzie down the aisle. Paul left her by the bridesmaids and took his place with the groomsmen. Suzie was relieved that the crime had been solved and everyone could relax.

Jason met Suzie's eyes with a smile of gratitude. Then all attention shifted to the bride. Summer stepped out on the side deck of Dune House with her arm wrapped around her father's. The sunlight caught the subtle jewels in her gown.

Each one sparkled as she began to walk towards Jason. That was what it looked like to Suzie. Summer's gaze didn't stray to her guests, to her father, or to any other family members. Her eyes locked to Jason's the moment she took that first step, and remained there as her father pressed her hand into Jason's. "I decided to add an inscription to our rings." He smiled at Summer. "I know that we've both weathered a lot. I know that as we move forward in life we will face a lot more. But just as the ring says, I know that no matter what, as long as we are together, we will make it."

"Through any storm." Summer blinked back tears as she read the inscription. "Yes, Jason, through any storm." She leaned forward and kissed him. The minister cleared his throat.

"Excuse me, it's not time for that yet."

Jason grinned as Summer blushed and pulled away. "Oh, it's always time for that." He winked at her. The crowd laughed and clapped. The minister blushed. As the ceremony continued Suzie's heart warmed with the hope of what might come next. Perhaps the week began with murder, but it was ending with the promise of a new beginning, and all of the joy that would come with it. And she had no doubt that the future held many more unexpected surprises.

The End

More Cozy Mysteries by Cindy Bell

Dune House Cozy Mysteries

Seaside Secrets

Boats and Bad Guys

Treasured History

Hidden Hideaways

Dodgy Dealings

Suspects and Surprises

Ruffled Feathers

Chocolate Centered Cozy Mysteries

The Sweet Smell of Murder

A Deadly Delicious Delivery

A Bitter Sweet Murder

A Treacherous Tasty Trail

Sage Gardens Cozy Mysteries

Birthdays Can Be Deadly

Money Can Be Deadly

Trust Can Be Deadly

Ties Can Be Deadly

Rocks Can Be Deadly

Jewelry Can Be Deadly

Wendy the Wedding Planner Cozy Mysteries

Matrimony, Money and Murder

Chefs, Ceremonies and Crimes

Knives and Nuptials

Mice, Marriage and Murder

Heavenly Highland Inn Cozy Mysteries

Murdering the Roses

Dead in the Daisies

Killing the Carnations

Drowning the Daffodils

Suffocating the Sunflowers

Books, Bullets and Blooms

A Deadly serious Gardening Contest

A Bridal Bouquet and a Body

Bekki the Beautician Cozy Mysteries

Hairspray and Homicide

A Dyed Blonde and a Dead Body

Mascara and Murder

Pageant and Poison

Conditioner and a Corpse

Mistletoe, Makeup and Murder

Hairpin, Hair Dryer and Homicide

Blush, a Bride and a Body

Shampoo and a Stiff

Cosmetics, a Cruise and a Killer

Lipstick, a Long Iron and Lifeless

Camping, Concealer and Criminals

Treated and Dyed

Made in the USA
Columbia, SC
18 June 2020

11370329R00157